AF241823

SLIMBIES: GIRL
A Gift in the Dark

D. R. Long

drlongwrites.com

For Girl,

and all the great puppers out there.

Dogs are family. Bring them inside.

Part 1

Chapter I

She sat in the window of the pet store. Her chocolate eyes met Evan's, and that was all it took.

"Well aren't you just adorable," Evan said, barely audible.

The air in the mall carried that strange mix of the season. Stale coffee from the food court, sweet cinnamon pretzels, the sharp bite of disinfectant. Holiday music played tinny from overhead speakers, but it couldn't cover the undertone of sweat and stale coats, the smell of too many people packed together, trying to pretend things were normal.

He stopped in the current of shoppers, the Lego Store bag crinkling in his hand. That was all he'd managed for the kids so far. One small set apiece, the kind that would take an hour to build and maybe a day before the pieces were scattered underfoot. Not much of a Christmas, but it was something.

Money was tight. Society felt like it was crumbling. He felt both pressing in on him every time he opened his wallet, every time he stepped into a store. Shelves half-stocked, prices climbing, people glaring like survival was a competition. Christmas was supposed to mean joy, but this year it just felt like keeping the walls from caving in.

He couldn't fix any of it. Not really, but maybe he could give the kids a day where it didn't matter. One morning with wrapping paper on the floor, a couple toys on the table, laughter that sounded real. Something to prove they still had a family, even if the world outside was falling apart.

The pup pressed against the glass, nose leaving a fogged circle. Dirty white fur matted, ribs a little sharp beneath her coat. A discount tag hung on the corner of the window like a silent dare. SALE. Like they couldn't even give her away.

"It would be nice to give them a little more..." he muttered under his breath.

Evan rubbed the back of his neck. With everything going on right now... a dog was the last thing they needed. More mouths to feed, more noise, more worry. Mara would kill him for even thinking about it.

But the kids... the kids could use a distraction. Something warm to hold, something to care about. Just until this thing blew over. However long that might take.

His chest tightened. He stayed there longer than he should have, watching the pup's eyes track his every twitch. She pawed once at the glass, small claws squeaking, like she already belonged to them.

Evan forced himself to look away, shaking his head. "No way," he muttered. He adjusted the Lego Store bag and pushed back into the crowd. "Still," he added under his breath, "Lena would've loved a dog like that."

Evan pushed deeper into the current of shoppers, shoulder to shoulder with strangers, all of them clinging to bags like lifelines. He angled toward the grocery at the far end of the concourse, head down, Lego Store bag crinkling at his side. Somewhere above the noise of the crowd, the mall PA crackled to life, bright and cheery as a game-show host.

"TrimLife - the miracle in a bottle! Shed stubborn weight, fast and safe, just in time for the holidays!"

"They don't tell you how much it makes you shit..." His thoughts interrupted when a woman beside him snorted and patted her stomach. "But I guess I could use another bottle myself."

A man a few steps over, a heavyset guy in a puffy winter coat, latched onto the line like it was the best joke he'd heard all year. "Guess I could too!" he called out, repeating it for his buddy. The laughter that followed was loud, sharp, brittle. It spread down the line of shoppers like static, but nobody's eyes looked any lighter for it. Even the man who laughed hardest had his jaw clenched too tight when it was over.

Evan felt the unease ripple through the air, but he shook it off. He wasn't here to read faces. He was here to make Christmas happen, thin shelves or not. Mara would roll her eyes, sure, but he was going to bring something home for the kids. Something that proved they still had a family, even if the world outside the mall was cracking at the edges.

The noise of the crowd thinned as Evan passed the electronics store. A wall of televisions glowed against the concourse, every set tuned to the same urgent feed. A small cluster formed, half horrified, half entertained. He slowed without meaning to, drawn in by the flashing lights and the sharp edge of panic in the anchors' voices.

Grainy cell phone footage filled the screens: police cruisers scattered through a city park, sirens wailing, yellow tape flapping in the wind. Medics crouched over someone on the ground, their gloves slick, moving with frantic, jerking motions. The crawl at the bottom screamed: MAN BITES ANOTHER MAN IN UNPROVOKED ATTACK - VICTIM IN CRITICAL CONDITION.

Then came the clip. Shaky, blurred, but brutal in its clarity. A man was straddling another figure in the grass, shoulders pumping like an animal tearing into prey. His head came up once, chin and lips drenched dark red, something stringy hanging from his teeth before he bent down again. The phone mic caught a wet, tearing sound followed by the shriek of someone just off-camera. The attacker didn't flinch. He shook his head like a dog ripping meat from a bone.

The camera jolted sideways, showing just a slice of the man's face as police swarmed. His eyes were wide, rolling, foam and blood smeared together at the corners of his mouth. One officer struck him with a baton and he barely reacted, lunging again before the feed cut away.

Evan stood frozen, frown carved deep. "Jesus Christ..."

A teenaged boy near the glass grinned wide. "Zombie apocalypse!" he shouted.

The girl holding his hand pulled his arm away, "Stop it, Aiden! It's not funny."

"Oh what's wrong? You scared of the slim zombies? The slimbies? Oooohhhh! They're gonna eat ya!" He laughed as he tried to tickle her. She squealed in a shrill scream while trying to wrestle away from him.

Evan muttered under his breath, shaking his head as he pushed back into the current of shoppers. "World gone crazy."

As he pushed deeper into the concourse, the mall felt wrong. Holiday lights shimmered too bright, almost buzzing at the edges of his vision. Shoppers' smiles stretched too sharp, their laughter ringing hollow, like everyone was forcing cheer just to keep from cracking. The cinnamon-sweet air sat heavy in his chest, cloying instead of warm.

He adjusted the Lego Store bag, forced himself into the stream of shoppers. He made it halfway to the doors before stopping dead. The thought of Christmas morning... The kids tearing through paper, finding nothing but a couple boxes of bricks. It hit him like a gut punch. Maybe Mara would kill him. Maybe it was stupid. But maybe stupid was what they all needed right now.

Evan squared his shoulders. He'd pull this Christmas off, no matter what. Mara could scold, the shelves could empty, the world could come apart at the seams... But his kids would have one good morning, one bright spot to hang onto. He'd give damn near anything to see them smile like they used to.

He stood there a long moment, jaw tight, then muttered under his breath:

"Fuck it. The kids deserve something good."

He turned, shouldering back against the tide, heading straight for the pet store window.

Chapter II

The garage door creaked shut behind him, the cold air giving way to the warmer, lived-in breath of the house. The place smelled faintly of pine from the half-leaning tree in the living room and the sharp bite of onion and garlic from the kitchen. A modest single-family home, walls close but not suffocating, cozy in that stretched-thin way that showed everything had been patched, reused, or held together with good intentions. A string of lights sagged across the front window, a few bulbs dead, the rest buzzing a little too bright. The counter carried the weight of a week's worth of clutter. Mail, school papers, a broken ornament waiting for glue. Nothing was perfect, but it was theirs.

Evan stepped inside, hands empty, his jacket damp with melted snow. He closed the door softly, as if even sound might give him away. Out in the garage, tucked in the backseat of the car, his real prize waited. "I'll have to bring out water for her." He pushed the thought down, straightened his shoulders, and crossed the threshold like any other night.

Mara stood at the stove, apron tied over a faded sweatshirt, hair pulled back in a messy knot. Steam curled from the pot in front of her as she stirred with slow, deliberate movements, the kind of focus born from stretching groceries into something that could pass for a holiday meal. She glanced up as he entered, tired but sharp-eyed, the kind of look that saw more than he wanted her to.

"Hey, sweetie," Evan said, leaning in to kiss her cheek. He gave her a quick wink. "You can be mad at me later. Just... don't go in the garage tonight."

Mara froze mid-stir, turned her head just enough to catch his grin. "Oh no. What did you do?"

"Nothing illegal," he offered, too quickly. "Probably."

She sighed through her nose, but there was the faintest curve at the corner of her mouth. "You're impossible."

"And yet, you still put up with me." He hung his coat and crossed the kitchen like a man who knew he'd been caught, but wasn't ready to admit how bad yet.

The living room glowed with the soft flicker of Christmas lights and the too-loud jingle of a holiday special. Wrapping paper scraps from earlier crafts littered the floor, and a half-toppled bowl of popcorn had left kernels scattered across the rug. On the couch cushions, Lena was curled up with her knees tucked, eyes sharp and skeptical even as she laughed at the cartoon. Noah sprawled on the carpet in front of her, chin propped on his fists, wide-eyed like the show was the most important thing in the world.

Evan stepped in, tossing his damp jacket on the arm of the chair as he took them in. For a heartbeat, just seeing them there was enough. A little bubble of warmth sealed off from the chaos he'd left behind at the mall.

"Hey, Dad!" Noah twisted around, grinning. "Did you get me one?"

Evan frowned in mock confusion. "One what?"

"A phone," Noah said, bouncing up to his knees. "Come on, you were out shopping..."

Evan snorted and dropped onto the couch, patting his son's shoulder as he passed. "You'll get one when you're driving, not a day before. You know the deal."

Noah groaned and flopped back on the carpet, arms splayed. "That's like forever."

"Forever's a good thing," Evan said, leaning back and tugging Lena into a half-cuddle. "Means I still get to keep you around a while."

Lena tilted her head up at him, sly grin already forming. "So when do I get one?"

"Never," Evan said without missing a beat. His fingers darted to her ribs, making her squirm and giggle. "How else are we supposed to keep all the boys away?"

She squealed, laughing as she wriggled free. "Dad! Gross!"

For a moment, the house felt right. Just laughter, popcorn, and a cartoon glowing too bright against the walls.

The cartoon sputtered mid-song, Rudolph's nose frozen in a red smear of static. The screen blinked black, then the jarring beep of the Emergency Broadcast System cut through the room. The kids flinched, covering their ears.

"It's so loud!" Lena whined.

The seal of the Department of Public Health appeared, grainy and official. A flat, monotone voice followed, without inflection, as though read from a script:

"Attention. Reports of severe adverse reactions to TrimLife and other name brand injections. Symptoms include aggression, disorientation, and violent behavior. Citizens are advised to remain indoors and avoid contact with individuals displaying these symptoms. This is a precautionary measure."

From the kitchen doorway, Mara appeared, wiping her hands on a dish towel. She didn't say anything, just stood there, eyes fixed on the screen, her lips pressed thin. The light from the television washed her face in pale blue, making the shadows under her eyes seem deeper.

Evan shifted in his seat, suddenly aware of the sweat prickling at the back of his neck. His arm tightened unconsciously around Lena's shoulders. He forced a small laugh, too light, too quick.

"It's nothing," he said, waving vaguely at the screen. "They always make it sound worse than it is. Couple days, it'll pass."

The broadcast cut as abruptly as it started, Rudolph snapping back to life, belting his song like nothing had happened. The kids exchanged glances, nervous, unsure if they should keep watching or ask questions. Noah opened his mouth, but Evan ruffled his hair before he could speak.

"Don't worry about it," he said, leaning forward to grab a handful of popcorn. "Santa's still coming tonight. That's all that matters."

Mara didn't move. She kept her eyes on the screen for another long moment, then finally turned away, the towel clenched tight in her hand.

Dinner was simple. Pasta and sauce stretched thin, garlic bread made from the end of a loaf. Mara had lit a single candle in the middle of the table, not for romance but because one of the overhead bulbs had burned out weeks ago and they hadn't gotten around to replacing it. The flickering light made shadows jump across the walls, too restless for comfort.

Noah twirled his fork noisily, then blurted, "So... what's TrimLife? Is it like Santa pills?"

Lena giggled, nearly snorting milk out of her nose. "Santa pills! That's silly. Santa doesn't take pills, he eats cookies."

"Yeah," Noah shot back, grinning. "Maybe it's diet cookies so he can fit down chimneys."

Mara's fork stilled. She set it down carefully, eyes flicking to Evan. Her voice was low, measured, but it carried weight.

"Aggression and violent behavior? That's more than a side effect."

"Oh come on now. Look at me! Hasn't made me aggressive, has it?" Evan wiped his mouth with a napkin, stalling. He forced an easy shrug. "It's probably just panic. People overreact, the news blows it up... couple days, they'll clear it up. You'll see."

Mara didn't answer right away. She leaned back, arms crossed, studying him. Finally she muttered, "We should keep the doors locked tonight."

"We always keep them locked," Evan countered lightly. He reached for his glass, pretending not to notice the sweat on his temple. "Nothing to worry about."

Noah rolled his eyes. "So you're saying it is Santa pills. Got it."

Evan chuckled, but it was hollow, stretched too thin. "Don't worry about it. Christmas is tomorrow." He raised his fork, forcing cheer back onto the table. "And tomorrow means presents."

The kids lit up at that, their chatter tumbling over each other's. For a minute the kitchen filled with laughter again, but Mara's silence hung heavier than any noise.

After dinner, the kids were still arguing over who got the last breadstick when Evan pushed back his chair.

"I'll be right back," he said, casual, reaching for his coat. "Forgot something in the garage."

Mara's eyes tracked him as he moved toward the door. She didn't say a word, but the way her hand stilled on the dish towel spoke louder than anything.

The garage light hummed as he pulled the chain, spilling a weak yellow glow over boxes and tools stacked high against the walls. His breath fogged in the chill.

In the backseat of the car, the puppy stirred, lifting her head just enough for her chocolate eyes to meet his. She gave a soft whine, then curled tighter into the blanket he'd tucked around her.

Evan rested a hand on the cold metal of the doorframe, voice dropping to a whisper meant for no one but her. "Just a few days," he murmured. "Couple days and it all blows over. You'll see."

The pup blinked, slow and trusting, as if she believed him.

Chapter III

The sirens came first, thin and distant at the edges of the night. They rose and fell in Doppler arcs, slicing through the warmth of the living room like cold knives. Noah sat cross-legged on the carpet, half-listening to the TV's tinny jingle and half-tracking the wail outside. He glanced toward the window, but the glow of Christmas lights strung along the eaves blurred the dark beyond into a dull red-green haze.

Then the crash hit. A metallic shriek followed by the hollow boom of glass shattering. A car alarm ripped to life, echoing sharp and frantic down the block.

Noah froze. His body moved before his mind caught up, bare feet padding across the rug, then the tile, then the cool wood floor by the front door. He pressed a finger into the curtain, peeling it back just enough to see.

The street outside wasn't quiet anymore.

A figure staggered into the spill of a streetlamp, jerky and angular, like his bones didn't know how to carry him anymore. He lurched against a parked sedan and then began slamming his fists down onto the hood. The metal dented with each blow, alarm screaming louder.

Noah's stomach turned. The man wasn't big. In fact, he was impossibly thin. His jacket hung from his frame like wet laundry, sleeves slipping back to reveal arms roped with veins that bulged against bone. Every strike of his fists looked like it should break them, but he just kept hitting, faster and harder, his head jerking side to side as if his neck couldn't hold still.

When he finally looked up, Noah's breath caught in his throat. The man's jaw opened too far, unhinged like a snake, lips drawn back until his gums showed raw and pink. He screamed at the night, a sound too wet, too ragged, half-growl, half-gurgle. Dark spit flew from his mouth, and under the orange light Noah swore he saw something stringy dangling between his teeth.

The words slipped out of him before he could think, soft as a prayer. "They're not dead. Just emptied."

A hand touched his shoulder. He screamed a short high yip, spinning, only to find his mother's face inches from his. Mara's eyes were wide but steady, her voice low and firm. "Back from the window."

He didn't argue. "Yes, mama. Sorry." She pulled the curtain closed and guided him away, her fingers tight on his arm, knuckles white.

Behind them, the car alarm howled, joined by another and another, until the whole street seemed to scream.

The house held a fragile kind of silence, the kind that left you uneasy. Every tick of the wall clock sounded like a hammer in the stillness. Outside, the neighborhood was darker than it should have been, the streetlamps hazy through the cold, like the air itself wanted to hide what was happening out there.

Mara sat in the living room with the kids bundled under blankets on the couch. Lena's small hand curled tight against her brother's sweatshirt as they slept side by side, a fortress of pillows around them. Mara had insisted they stay downstairs tonight after the accident that had startled Noah. Too far, too risky to leave them tucked away in their rooms, where she couldn't reach them fast enough if something went wrong. She wanted them close. Close where she could count their breaths.

Evan was planted by the front door with a bat across his knees. He looked like a sentry, but one that had been carved out of wax. His head kept drooping forward, chin nearly touching his chest, then jerking up again. A dark sheen of sweat ran down from his hairline, catching the dim light. The fabric of his shirt clung damp to his back and underarms, plastered there like he'd been running laps instead of sitting still. His right leg twitched every few seconds, heel tapping the floor in a nervous rhythm.

Mara watched him for a long time before she reached out, laying the lightest touch on his shoulder.

He snapped upright like she'd lit a fire under him, eyes wild, bat lifting halfway into the air before he realized it was her. His knuckles whitened on the grip before he lowered it, breath harsh through his nose.

"You should rest," she said, keeping her voice soft. "I'll keep watch."

His jaw tightened. His voice came out low, rough. "Stop fucking worrying. I'm fine."

The words were sharp enough to sting the air between them. He caught himself, eyes flicking away, but the damage hung there anyway. Mara didn't respond. She just studied him in silence, her lips pressed thin, the unease hardening in her stomach.

Then came the sound.

Something moved in the yard. Not walking, not running, but skittering. Quick bursts followed by dragging pauses. Shadows flitted across the curtains, strange and too long. Mara stood, body stiff, and positioned herself between the window and the couch where the kids slept.

The noise came closer. A shape scraped along the siding, then a breath... ragged and wet, fogged the glass. A face pressed against the window, pale skin stretched too tight across cheekbones, lips peeled back to bare its teeth. The pane clouded with each rattling gasp, then cleared, then clouded again.

Lena stirred in her sleep. Noah mumbled something and shifted under the blanket. Mara held her breath and kept her hand raised, ready to press them both down if they woke.

The figure smeared its cheek against the glass, teeth clicking once against it, before it lurched backward into the dark, vanishing as quickly as it had come.

For a long beat, the only sound in the room was the car alarm still bleating faintly down the block. Then, muffled through the walls, came a single sharp, high-pitched yip from the garage.

Mara's head twitched in that direction, breath caught, but Evan didn't so much as flinch. The kids stirred under their blankets and settled again, none the wiser. The sound died, swallowed by the dark.

Silence returned, heavier than before.

Across the room, Evan muttered, almost to himself. "I'm fine. It's fine." His voice cracked on the last word, and Mara wasn't sure if he was talking to her or to something inside his own skin.

Part 2

Chapter IV

The first light of morning slipped through the blinds and stretched across the living room, striping over the couch where the kids had fallen asleep. Lena's arm dangled toward the floor, her cheek mashed into a pillow, while Noah's legs stuck out from the blanket they'd been fighting over all night. The tree in the corner glowed weakly, its bulbs mismatched, half of them blinking out of rhythm. The lights lit their faces in flashes of red and green, a soft shimmer against the stillness.

For a moment, it almost looked like Christmas was going to feel normal. There were a few wrapped boxes leaned against the stand, none of them large, none of them extravagant. Maybe more promise than present, but something to distract the kids from the terrors happening outside.

In the kitchen, Mara sat hunched at the table, robe pulled tight across her shoulders, steam rising from the chipped mug between her hands. Her eyes were ringed with the kind of tired that didn't go away with sleep, but she held herself steady. She always did.

Across from her, Evan cradled his own glass of coffee like it was something stronger, rolling it in his palm before taking a sip. He froze mid-swallow, nose wrinkling.

"Tastes funny," he muttered, then frowned deeper. "How long's this been sitting? Tastes like it's got... lemon. Mint. Rotten meat. I don't know what it is, but it's bad."

Mara lifted her mug and took a careful sip, swallowing without hesitation. She raised an eyebrow. "Tastes fine to me."

Evan stared into the dark swirl a second longer, as if the answer might rise from the bottom, then set the glass down harder than he meant to. Coffee sloshed over the rim, streaking the table. He rubbed at his temple with the heel of his hand.

From the living room, the tree lights flickered against the wall. Beneath them, front and center, sat a red box with a fat ribbon tied in a bow. It didn't look like the others. Too bright, too deliberate. From inside came the faintest whimper, followed by the scratch of a tiny paw against cardboard.

Mara's gaze drifted toward it, her mouth pressed into a flat line. Evan didn't look up.

A rustle broke the quiet. On the couch, Lena stirred first, hair a tangled halo in the tree's glow. She stretched her arms wide, a little yawn squeaking out. Noah woke rubbing his eyes with balled fists before blinking toward the pile of presents. For a moment, both of them just sat there blinking, faces washed in the shifting red-and-green glow, as if the lights themselves had pulled them awake.

Mara slipped into the room, setting her mug on the end table before easing herself down into the armchair. She smoothed her robe and watched her children in the half-dark, lips pressed together but softening at the sight.

Evan appeared in the doorway, one shoulder propped against the frame. His eyes lingered on the kids like he was memorizing them. A crooked grin stretched slow across his face, twitching at the edges like it didn't quite belong there, but he caught it, forcing warmth into his face.

Then came the sound.

A sharp, muffled bark from the big red box.

The kids froze.

Both of their faces lit soft by the blinking bulbs, eyes sharpening as the whimper came again, sharper this time, followed by a muffled yip.

Noah's gasp cut through the room. "No way..."

Lena squealed, hands flying to her mouth. Noah shot to his feet, eyes wide. "Is it what I think it is?"

Mara looked at him across the room with daggers in her eyes. She mouthed the words "You didn't" at him.

His eyes fixed on the kids, Evan's grin spread wider, almost maniacal. "Go ahead." His voice caught in his throat, rough for a second before smoothing out. "Open it." He leaned forward just a fraction, and for an instant he almost looked ravenously hungry.

The kids didn't wait for another word. Lena lunged first, fingers tearing at the ribbon until the bow came loose and fluttered to the floor. Noah yanked the lid aside, cardboard scraping against the rug.

Inside, a small bundle of fur trembled in the dim light. The puppy blinked hard, ears too big for her head, ribs showing sharp under a patchy coat. All white except for one tan ear, a faded pink collar hanging loose around her neck like it had been meant for someone else's dog.

She let out a soft whimper and stumbled forward on oversized paws, then collapsed right into Lena's waiting arms.

"Ohhh my God," Lena breathed, rocking her like a baby. The puppy buried her nose under the girl's chin, still shaking.

Noah hovered close, hand out as if guarding them both. "She needs water," he said quickly, scanning the room like he'd fetch a bowl right that second. "And food. Something. Anything."

"Her name's Lucy," Lena declared, voice sure, like she'd already decided.

Noah's head snapped up. "Star," he countered. "She should be Star. Something... I don't know, something that means we'll always find our way."

"Lucy is cuter."

"Star is stronger. Or what about Raven?"

"No, Cherry!"

"That doesn't even make sense!"

The debate sparked and swirled, neither willing to budge, both clutching the little life in their own way.

From the armchair, Mara rose slowly. He smile faded, her eyes lingered on the puppy a moment longer, unreadable. Then she turned, gaze sliding to Evan. Without a word, she tilted her head toward the kitchen.

Evan swallowed, jaw tight, and followed her as the kids kept arguing in the glow of the tree.

From the kitchen doorway, Mara's voice cut across the laughter in the living room. "More mouths to feed, more noise. This house isn't a kennel, Evan."

He didn't even let her finish. "Let them have this," he snapped, harsher than he meant to, the words cracking out like a whip. "Goddammit, Mara. We could barely give them gifts this year."

The mug trembled in his grip, liquid sloshing near the rim. He clenched it tighter, knuckles white, as though forcing himself to keep it together.

"Calm down, honey. I know you mean well. We really just can't afford the dog. No matter how cute she is." Mara said very calmly, her shoulders relaxing against the wall.

Silence settled in the room, thick and ugly. From the TV in the corner came the drone of a newscaster: "Authorities are reporting multiple unprovoked attacks in Wilmington... families are urged to remain inside... avoid anyone displaying erratic or violent behavior..."

The screen flickered with shaky footage of yellow police tape snapping in the wind, sirens strobing red and blue, a gurney wheeled into an ambulance.

Mara's hands tightened around her robe belt. She stared at the footage, unsettled, a low pit opening in her stomach.

Evan's jaw twitched. His breath came fast, his face slick with sweat. Then he barked, louder, sudden: "Turn that shit off. It's fucking Christmas."

The words hit the room like a door slamming shut. His eyes were too wide, his grip too tight, as though something inside him was straining at the seams.

"Evan, are you oka-" Mara started.

Just then, the kids bolted into the kitchen, the puppy wriggling between their arms, laughter spilling bright and oblivious. The moment cracked, tension smothered under their joy. But Mara's gaze lingered on Evan, watching the shadow flicker behind his smile.

The room calmed, but only on the surface. Mara pressed her lips into a thin line, crossed to the counter, and switched the channel without a word. A cartoon flickered on in place of the news, tinny jingles filling the silence. She didn't argue. She didn't need to, her eyes spoke enough.

On the rug, Noah cradled the pup against his chest, her tiny ribs fluttering with each fast breath. He bent close, whispering into the soft fur. "Don't worry. I'll keep you safe."

Lena tugged at her brother's sleeve, her voice bright. "She's not a Star. She's not a Lucy or a Sammi or a Nola. She's a Moon."

Noah frowned, thought about it, then gave a little shrug. "Moon is good."

The pup gave a tiny yip, as though she agreed.

Evan reached down, tugging gently at the collar around her neck. The faded tag clinked as he held it up to the light: GOOD GIRL etched in cheap, scuffed letters. He pulled a marker from the drawer, uncapped it, and scrawled a new name across the metal.

MOON

He clipped it back on and let it dangle against her fur, the old word still faint beneath the new one.

Evan slumped into his chair again, sweat beading at his temples, eyes staring past the tree lights like he wasn't really in the room.

Mara's voice came flat, resigned. "I'll make breakfast."

Chapter V

The house smelled like Christmas, stubbornly so. Sausage hissed in the skillet, cheap pancake batter bubbled on the griddle, eggs crackled in the pan. Mara moved through it all with her sleeves shoved past her elbows, hair tied back, determination stamped into her tired face.

If the world outside was falling apart, then in here, even if only just for a morning... she was going to hold the seams together. Even if she had to do it alone.

The table was set as best as she could manage: mismatched plates, plastic cups, a candle stub flickering bravely at the center. Lena and Noah came barreling in at the smell, hair tangled from sleep, voices bouncing over one another. Moon scampered at their heels, paws skidding on the kitchen tile.

"Pancakes!" Noah shouted, sliding into his chair.

"Not just pancakes, there's sausage too," Lena said, like she'd discovered treasure. She leaned down to scoop Moon into her lap. "Can she sit with us? Please?"

Mara shot her a look. "The dog does not get a chair."

"But it's Christmas," Lena pressed, hugging Moon tighter.

"Christmas or not, she eats on the floor," Mara said, but her voice lacked bite.

Evan followed them in, slower, heavier. He sat with a thump, sweat already shining along his temple, jaw tight as if every step had been work. Still, his eyes sharpened at the sight of food, fixed hungrily on the platter as Mara set it down.

For a moment, it almost felt normal. Syrup spilling too quickly, pancakes ripped into uneven halves, eggs shoved around plates while Moon stretched from the floor to lick a drizzle of syrup that had escaped. Mara pretended not to notice, even smiled faintly.

Evan forked into a sausage, chewing like it was the only thing on the table worth eating. The pancakes and eggs cooled untouched on his plate.

"These are a little overcooked," he muttered finally, words flat, forcing a crooked half-smile to soften it. "Freezer burn maybe?"

Noah glanced up, mouth already sticky with syrup. "They taste good to me."

"Best pancakes ever," Lena added quickly, grinning at Mara before turning to whisper into Moon's fur, "You don't know what you're missing."

Evan rubbed at his temple with the heel of his hand, staring down at his plate like it was daring him. The smile never reached his eyes.

For a while, the clatter of forks and the syrupy chatter of the kids filled the space. Then, almost without warning, Evan's voice cut in.

"You know," he said, leaning back in his chair, fork dangling in his hand, "one Christmas when I was about your age... I got a truck. Bright yellow. Biggest thing I ever saw." His eyes gleamed like he could still see it under some long-forgotten tree.

The kids perked up, chewing slower, listening.

"Had these big wheels," Evan went on, gesturing with both hands. "Could roll it over anything. Snow, mud, didn't matter. Toughest truck in the world."

But then his words faltered. His brow furrowed, like he was fighting to catch the memory before it slipped through his fingers.

"Or... no. It wasn't a truck. It was a car. Green one. Little racecar with stripes. Yeah. I used to push it around the floor for hours..." His voice trailed again.

The shift was so abrupt even the kids noticed. Lena frowned, lowering her fork. Noah glanced at her, eyes narrowed, like checking if she'd caught it too.

He blinked hard, like trying to reset himself, then gave a short, jagged laugh. "No. No, it was a bike. Red bike. Brightest thing on the block. Couldn't keep me off it."

Mara's eyes lingered on him longer than the kids'. She tilted her head slightly, concern tugging at the corners of her mouth. He wasn't just mixing up details like anyone might. There was a fog in his voice, a stutter in the rhythm that didn't belong to nostalgia. She tightened her grip on her coffee mug, knuckles whitening as she studied him, but she said nothing yet.

Evan kept talking, but now it felt like words spilling without shape. "Best Christmas of my life. Best. I rode that car, the truck, I mean... rode it all day long."

The table went quiet. Only the candle flickered, wax sliding down in uneven rivers.

Mara reached across, laying her hand gently near his. Her voice was steady but low, as if speaking to someone on a ledge. "That sounds nice, Evan. Why don't you let the kids play with Moon now? Maybe you should lie down for a while."

Evan's jaw tightened. His eyes snapped to hers, too sharp, too quick. He slammed his palm against the table. Not hard enough to spill plates, but loud enough to make the kids flinch. His teeth clenched so hard they groaned.

"I'm fine. Don't fucking worry, Mara."

The words came out fast, clipped, leaving the silence heavier than before. Noah froze with his fork halfway to his mouth. Lena curled her arms tighter around Moon, who gave a nervous whimper. Mara didn't move her hand, but her eyes stayed locked on him, reading the cracks spreading just beneath the surface.

The radio crackled, breaking through the clatter of dishes with the piercing, sterile tone of the Emergency Broadcast System. The sound cut through the house like a blade, bouncing off the walls, too loud, too shrill to ignore.

"New reports confirm symptoms include aggression, disorientation, and uncontrollable hunger. Families are urged to remain indoors. Do not approach anyone displaying these symptoms-"

"I thought I'd said to turn that shit off!" Evan's voice erupted over the broadcast.

"No, I wanna hear it," Noah blurted, leaning forward on his elbows, eyes wide at the voice on the speaker. His fork clattered against his plate as he reached toward the radio.

Evan's chair shrieked across the floor, wood scraping hard against linoleum. He lurched upright in a violent motion that made the candle flame jump. His jaw flexed, spit glistening at the corners of his mouth. "I said turn that shit off! It's Christmas!" he roared, the words rattling the dishes left on the counter.

The kids froze, forks halfway to their mouths. Mara's hand shot out, pulling Lena into her side with a reflexive grip, her knuckles whitening as she held her daughter close. "Evan-" she began...

Evan's face twisted into something almost unrecognizable, veins raised like cords along his neck, his eyes too bright, too sharp. With a guttural sound, he swung his arm and drove the table sideways. It crashed into the wall with a splintering crack, plates skittering and shattering across the floor. Food smeared in greasy streaks, syrup dripping down the paneling like blood. The candle toppled, wax pooling fast across the table's edge before Mara caught it upright again.

The kids shrieked, clutching each other, their chairs tipping as they scrambled backward. Moon yelped, tail tucked, scrambling behind Noah's legs.

Foam bubbled at the corners of Evan's lips as he staggered toward the radio, breath tearing in and out of his chest in savage, uneven gasps. His hand slammed down on the dial, twisting hard enough the plastic squealed. He wrenched it back and forth, but the voice kept droning through the static, louder, sharper, as if it were burrowing into the very air of the house itself.

"...aggression, disorientation, uncontrollable hunger. Families are urged-"

Evan's fingers slipped, shaking too violently to find their hold. His nails scraped across the knobs, drawing sparks of sound. A strangled snarl tore from his throat as he pounded the side of the radio with his fist, again and again, the casing rattling on the counter.

And still, the broadcast carried on, a flat, merciless voice echoing above the chaos.

Mara moved fast, stepping around the mess, her hand steady on the dial as she clicked the radio off. The silence that followed rang louder than the broadcast, as if the whole house were holding its breath. She forced her voice into a calm she didn't feel.

"Evan. Please. Just... come lay down."

Evan's hands stayed locked on the counter, knuckles bone-white, chest rising and falling in ragged jerks. The Christmas lights flickered off the tree, shadows jittering across his face. For a heartbeat, Mara thought he'd blow again, that he'd hurl the radio or come at her with his bare hands.

Then something shifted. His shoulders sagged, the fury leaking out of him all at once. He shook his head as if trying to clear it, eyes unfocused. "Sorry," he muttered, voice raw and distant. "I didn't mean... I'm sorry guys..."

He pushed himself upright, but his steps wobbled, uneven, his frame bent like he'd aged ten years in a minute. He didn't look at Mara. He didn't look at the kids. Just shuffled past them, jaw tight, disappearing down the hall with the bedroom door clicking shut behind him. The sound carried like a gavel strike.

Mara's exhale trembled, the only sound in the kitchen. She turned to the kids, who clutched each other tight, Moon pressed nervously between their knees, the pup's ears slicked flat against her head. "Go play in the living room," Mara said softly. "Take Moon."

They nodded fast, eager to obey, scampering off with whispered reassurances into the dog's fur. Moon settled quickly, curling in Lena's lap, her pink collar catching the glow of the tree lights as her tail thumped once against the floor before stilling.

Mara stayed behind, hands braced on the counter as if the wood alone was holding her up. Her eyes drifted to the table, to the mess splattered on the wall and on the floor, a pile of eggs glossed with cooling grease, a single sausage chewed halfway through and abandoned. Syrup congealed in the ridges of the tile floor, sticky and untouched.

She stared at it for a long time, the weight of the silence pressing in, her reflection warped in the syrup's dark pool. The smell of breakfast lingered heavy in the air, but instead of warmth it carried the sour edge of dread.

Chapter VI

Daylight crept in as the morning crawled by, pale and sluggish through the blinds, as if the sun itself didn't want to come all the way inside. The house felt smaller than it had before, walls pressing closer, shadows stretching longer than they should. Even the tree in the corner looked wrong, its lights throwing jagged patterns across the carpet.

Noah sat cross-legged on the couch with Moon in his lap, trying to keep still, but his eyes kept tracking Dad. Back and forth. Back and forth. Evan's steps thudded against the floor, uneven and restless, like he couldn't find the right rhythm. His T-shirt clung dark under the arms, chest damp, strands of hair plastered to his forehead. He muttered to himself in a low rasp that made the air seem colder, words swallowed before Noah could catch them.

It wasn't just the pacing. It was the way he snapped at little things. When Lena hummed under her breath, a Christmas song stuck in her head, Evan's head jerked toward her like she'd screamed. When the TV crackled with static between commercials, his jaw tightened, teeth grinding loud enough for Noah to hear from across the room. Even Moon, nails ticking lightly against the hardwood, drew a sharp curse: "Christ, will someone shut that damn noise up? We just got the damn dog and it's already driving me crazy!"

Noah's chest felt tight, like he couldn't pull in enough air. He hugged the pup closer, burying his face in her fur to steady himself. Moon squirmed but stayed.

"It's okay, Moon," he whispered to her.

His dad wasn't just mad. He wasn't just tired. There was something wrong in the way his eyes didn't blink enough, in the way his lips twitched at the corners like he was chewing on something invisible.

Noah whispered it, so quiet he wasn't sure if Lena even heard from the floor by the tree.

"He's not okay."

She'd heard, the look in her eyes said she had.

And in Noah's eyes, everything about his father seemed too loud, too dangerous, filling the room with a weight no one knew how to lift.

Moon squatted by the back door, tail wagging like she'd done something right. A little puddle spread across the floorboards, harmless, ordinary.

"Moon! No! We go potty outside," Lena picked the puppy up, showing her the backyard.

Evan's head snapped toward it. His face twisted, red flooding his neck in an instant.

"Goddammit!" His voice ripped out raw. He slammed his fist into the wall, the sound sharp and hollow. Moon yelped, curling into Lena's arms. The kids both screamed.

He spun, lunging, hands curled like claws.

"No!" Noah's voice cracked, but his body moved anyway, planting himself between his father and Lena and the dog. His arms went wide, heart hammering in his throat.

Evan's eyes locked onto him, red-rimmed and fever-bright. His hands clamped Noah's shoulders, iron hard, fingers digging deep until Noah thought the bone might snap. He shook him once, twice, teeth bared like he couldn't decide if he was growling or speaking.

"Dad... stop!" Noah gasped, trying to twist free. Evan's grip only tightened, knuckles white, nails scraping through the fabric, biting skin.

Mara burst forward, shoving herself between them, clawing at Evan's wrists. "Evan!!! NO! GET OFF!" Her voice cracked with panic. She yanked and pulled, throwing her full weight into it.

For a moment he didn't budge, body stiff as stone, breath hissing out like steam. Then, finally, something gave. His grip faltered just long enough for Noah to stumble back into Lena and the puppy.

Evan froze, chest heaving. His eyes twitched, the wildness folding inward but never leaving. His hands shook as he dragged them back to his sides.

Tears rolled down Noah and Lena's face, Mara forcing herself between Evan and the kids.

"I'm sorry..." The words came out wrong. Too flat. Too slow. His mouth twitched into something like a smile, but his eyes stayed hard. "It's okay. It's all okay... I just-" He dragged a breath that rattled. "I need to cool off."

He turned sharp, shoving past, yanking the door open. Cold air swept in, rattling the blinds. He stepped out, shoulders rigid, muttering to himself as the door banged shut behind him.

Mara stayed by the door a moment, hand on the frame, her chest rising and falling quick. She turned, looking at the kids. They clutched Moon between them, wide-eyed, silent, tears rolling. Mara didn't say a word. Her face said enough. It was etched in worry, lips pressed thin, eyes dark with fear. And then she followed Evan outside.

The screen door banged against its frame as Evan stalked out into the yard. His boots crunched the frost, pacing short, jagged circles in the brittle grass. His voice carried low and jagged, repeating like a broken record.

"I'm fine. I'm fine. I'm fine. I'm fine..."

Mara stayed in the doorway, one hand pressed hard against the wood, the other trembling at her side. She glanced back at the kids clinging together inside, then leaned down just enough to whisper.

"Something's wrong with your father."

Noah's jaw tightened. He wasn't a boy in that moment but something harder, older. His hand pulled Lena close, Lena holding Moon against her chest like a shield. He gave a single nod, teeth clenched.

Mara forced herself outside. The cold bit her cheeks, but her chest burned hotter with every step toward Evan. He had stopped pacing now, just standing in the yard with his shoulders heaving, staring at nothing.

"Evan," she said, careful, steady. "Tell me the truth. Did you have the shot?"

His head jerked toward her, too quick. "What shot?"

Her eyes narrowed. "The one all over the news. TrimLife. The weight-loss one."

Evan's jaw worked, chewing over words like they hurt to form. "Not everyone has those side effects," he muttered.

"But you are." Her voice cracked. She didn't shout, she didn't need to.

"I'm fine," he said again, sharper now, like that alone should be enough. His hands spread wide in mock calm, but his fingers twitched. "I promise. See? I'm calm now."

Mara stared at him, searching for the husband she knew beneath the sweat, the trembling, the raw edge in his eyes. Nothing came back but silence and shallow breath.

Finally, his shoulders sagged. He dropped his gaze to the ground. "Fine... Yeah. I took a couple. But just to try it, Mara. Just to look better for you and the kids. I know I put on a little weight this last year, and I thought..." His voice faltered. "I thought it might help."

"Oh, Evan..." Her chest tightened. Concern bloomed into something heavier, colder. It wasn't vanity, wasn't just bad luck... it was in him. Already eating him alive.

From down the street came a sudden honk, blaring through the frozen air. Then a scream. Sharp, real, tearing at the silence. Mara turned, her stomach hollowing, and looked back toward the house where the kids were still pressed against the window.

Evan followed her gaze, eyes darting. His voice dropped to a whisper. "Let's just... let's go back inside."

Together, they turned from the noise and walked toward the door. Mara's every step felt heavier than the last, her hand brushing her stomach as if to steady herself against the weight of what she already knew.

Mara stood at the window, one hand braced against the frame, her breath fogging the cold glass. Behind her, Evan had collapsed onto the couch, chest rising and falling in uneven swells, muttering under his breath as though even in half-sleep he was still arguing with shadows.

She kept her eyes outside. The daylight had started its slow fade, shadows stretching long and thin across the brittle yard. Everything out there felt brittle, like the air itself might crack if touched too hard.

Movement at the far end of the street snagged her attention. A shape staggering into view.

At first she thought it was just another neighbor, someone desperate to check the mail or shout across to a friend. But as it drew closer, details snapped into focus.

Skin clung to the figure in loose folds, hanging like melted wax, swinging with each jerky step. Some patches had gone soft and bubbled, splitting open so strips of flesh dangled, raw and wet against the winter air.

One leg dragged uselessly behind him, the shin bent at an impossible angle, but it didn't slow him. Each lurch carried him forward with unnatural speed, head twitching side to side like a dog scenting prey.

When he opened his mouth, the scream that ripped out was not human. The jaw hinged wider than it should, teeth snapping with a wet clack as spit flew into the cold.

Mara's stomach turned to stone.

The man... the husk... whatever he was, pitched sideways across the neighbor's yard and slammed against their front steps.

His hands clawed at the door, nails screeching deep grooves into the wood.

Inside, she saw curtains twitch. A light flick on. Then, disastrously, the door cracked open.

Mara's hand shot to her mouth. "No, Mr. Wallace..." she whispered, but it was already too late.

The skeletal figure lunged, slamming its weight against the frame, snarling through bared teeth. The door buckled under the strain, hinges groaning, the neighbor's panicked face vanishing behind it.

The sound of claw against wood filled the street, shrill and hungry.

Mara jerked the blinds down hard enough to rattle the frame, chest heaving. She pressed her palm flat against the wall, forcing her voice low and steady.

"Stay quiet," she whispered to the kids. "No matter what you hear. Just... stay quiet."

They huddled closer, Moon whimpering in Lena's arms.

Behind her, Evan was sprawled on the couch, one arm hanging limp over the side, his face slack with uneasy sleep. Sweat darkened the collar of his shirt, lips twitching in dreams.

Outside, the neighbor's scream cut through the brittle stillness, high and desperate. Mara froze, every muscle locked.

A gunshot split the air. Then another.

And then...

Silence.

The quiet that followed was worse than the noise.

Chapter VII

The television murmured in the background, another clipped warning cycling through: "Remain indoors. Do not engage. Symptoms include aggression, confusion, violent hunger," The words filled the room like static, ignored but impossible to tune out.

Evan shifted on the couch, a low groan pushing past his lips. Sweat slicked his skin, his shirt clinging like he'd been dragged from a storm. His chest rose shallow, stuttering, before he tried to push himself upright.

"Dad?" Noah's voice was small, cautious.

Evan muttered something. Slow, slurred, tangled words that Noah couldn't make out. His arm buckled under his own weight, and then he pitched forward. His body hit the carpet with a dull, heavy thud that seemed to shake the floor.

He let out one long, strained, slow wheeze that ended with a garbled gurgle.

Noah moved instantly, the instinct to help stronger than the fear biting at his stomach. But Mara's hand clamped down on his shoulder, fingers digging hard enough to hurt.

"Stay back," she hissed. "Something isn't right."

He looked up at her, confused, but the sharpness in her eyes kept him frozen. She wasn't looking at him. Her gaze was locked on Evan's body sprawled across the carpet.

For a long, terrible moment, Evan didn't move. His chest didn't rise. His eyes didn't open. He was still, pale, mouth slack. He looked less like a man passed out, more like a corpse left behind.

Noah felt his throat tighten. "Mom..." he whispered, but Mara's grip only tightened, her knuckles white against his shirt. She didn't answer. She just stared. "Mom, is he..."

"Shh..."

The house had never felt so quiet.

Lena slipped free of Mara's hand, too quick, too trusting. Her bare knees pressed into the carpet as she leaned close, voice trembling but soft.

"Daddy, it's okay..."

She reached out with small fingers, brushing sweat-clumped hair back from his clammy forehead. For a moment, Evan looked still, almost peaceful, like a body cooling in the silence.

His still body twitched, then his eyes snapped open.

They weren't his eyes. Not the brown Lena remembered. These were yellow, veined, and burning with animal hunger. His jaw cracked wide, unhinging too far, strings of spit stretching like webbing. A sound like bones grinding came out of him as his lips peeled back to expose teeth slick with saliva.

Before Mara could grab her daughter, before Noah could even gasp, Evan lunged upward.

His teeth sank into Lena's throat with a sound like ripping cloth and crunching celery stalks. Flesh split, cartilage snapped, and a geyser of blood sprayed across the living room carpet, hot enough that it steamed against the cold air spilling from the drafty window.

Lena screamed once, high and piercing. But it broke off into a choking gargle as blood bubbled from her mouth. Her tiny hands clawed frantically at Evan's face, nails raking his skin but slipping in the slick gore, smearing bright red across his cheeks and into his stubble.

Evan snarled like a starving dog, his head jerking side to side. Each wrench tore her further. Strings of gristle snapped between his teeth, veins stretched and ripped. A chunk of her trachea came loose with a wet pop, slapping onto the carpet. Blood pulsed from the wound in spurts, keeping time with her slowing heartbeat.

Mara screamed, hurling herself forward, yanking at his shoulders, nails raking skin... But Evan only clamped harder, jaw grinding like an animal tearing raw meat. His lips peeled back, froth and gore coating them. When he pulled his face up, Lena's throat was a ragged ruin, half-shredded, pumping blood in uneven bursts.

Noah pressed into the wall, clutching Moon. The puppy writhed and squealed, fur matted where blood mist had spattered onto them both. Noah whispered, shaking, "no no no no no," but the words were drowned in the wet sucking sound of Evan pulling another mouthful of flesh free.

Blood poured everywhere. Soaking Lena's pajamas, drenching Evan's shirt, dripping in fat rivulets from his chin onto the carpet. The smell of iron filled the room, thick and cloying, gagging Mara as she screamed again and again, her voice ripped raw from her throat: "LET HER GO!"

But he didn't.

Mara pulled herself back, stumbling over the overturned coffee table. Her pulse hammered so hard she could hear it in her ears as she sprinted for the kitchen.

The butcher block loomed in front of her, wood flecked with years of knife scars. Her hands shook so violently she almost missed the grip, but she wrapped both fists around the handle of the biggest blade and ripped it free. The clatter of the other knives toppling into the sink rang in her skull.

Blood smeared under her socks as she ran back, her foot skidding across the slick tile. She slammed shoulder-first into the doorway, steadying herself, and charged into the living room with a hoarse, breaking scream.

Evan was hunched over Lena, his face buried in her throat. The sound was unbearable. Not chewing, not biting, but a wet suctioning rip. Mara didn't think. She brought the knife up high, both hands locked on the handle, and drove it down into the back of his skull.

The blade punched through bone with a crack that vibrated up her arms. Evan jerked once, back arching, and then his whole body collapsed in a heavy sprawl beside his daughter. His jaw hung slack, the bite unfinished, blood still dripping from his chin onto her chest.

Lena choked in a widening pool, her voice a shredded gurgle of blood and air. "Mommy..." The word was thin, broken, drowned out by the bubbling rush from her torn throat that stained the carpet below. Mara dropped to her knees, the knife slipping from her grip with a dull thud.

She pressed trembling hands against the wound, but there was no stopping it. Her fingers came away painted red. Her sobs tore loose, frantic words tripping over themselves: "Hold on, baby, please, stay with me, please."

She gathered her daughter into her lap, but the warmth was fading too fast. Lena's body was already seizing. Her back arched violently, her limbs kicking against the floor in uneven spasms. Mara screamed her name, holding her shoulders down, but the convulsions only worsened.

And then...

Stillness.

For a breath, Lena lay limp, blood bubbling faintly at the open wound. Mara leaned closer, tears streaking her face.

Lena's body convulsed, limbs jerking like a puppet cut from its strings, eyes snapping open milky-white. Her throat wound gaped wider with every gasp. A guttural snarl rose from her small chest as she lunged upward, teeth bared, clawing for Mara's neck.

Mara shoved her down, tears streaking her face, trying to hold her by the shoulders. "Lena! Baby, it's me! Stop, please, it's me!" Her pleas cracked apart under the sound of her daughter hissing and thrashing, strength unnatural.

For a heartbeat Mara still fought to believe she could reach her. But the eyes staring back at her were gone - empty, hateful, wrong. Her gaze fell to the knife still clutched in her blood-slick hand.

Sobbing, she raised it and drove the blade into Lena's chest. The little body jerked but didn't stop. She did it again, and again. Still, Lena fought.

"Please..." Mara's voice broke as she twisted away, refusing to look. She raised the knife a final time and stabbed down, straight into her daughter's skull.

The thrashing ended in an instant. Just silence.

Mara crumpled forward over the tiny body, the knife still in her hand, her own breath coming in ragged, shuddering gasps.

Noah's wide eyes glistened in the half-light, his lips moving soundlessly, as though begging this not to be real.

The house reeked of iron and ruin. Blood smeared the walls, soaked into the carpet, still wet on Mara's trembling hands.

Mara's scream ripped through the house, her hands slick with blood, body shaking. She didn't stop to think, didn't stop to breathe. She shoved Noah toward the door, her voice ragged, "Run! Don't look back!"

Noah fumbled, grabbing his backpack from the hook by the door, Moon tucked trembling against his chest. His cheeks were streaked raw with tears, breath hitching in jagged bursts. He looked back once, just once, eyes wide and shattering. Then he bolted.

Mara stumbled after, bare feet slipping in her daughter and husband's blood, crimson smears left in her wake. Her robe flapped open in the cold draft, sticky with gore. She didn't seem to notice.

Across the street, the neighbor stood stiff in the yard, shotgun in his hands. He didn't move to help. Didn't call out. He just cocked the weapon, jaw set, eyes fixed on them like they were already lost.

Snow drifted down in slow, indifferent flakes, settling on the blood that trailed behind them. The world outside was silent except for the crunch of Noah's feet in the snow, the muffled whimper of the puppy against his chest.

Mara stumbled barefoot into the white, robe snapping in the wind, her breath rising in clouds. No coats. No shoes. No time.

The world outside was silent except for Noah's sobs and the puppy's whimper.

A mother and son, fled into the white, leaving everything they knew behind on Christmas Day.

Part 3

Chapter VIII

The snow came down thick, smothering sound, burying the
world in white. Wind cut across the drifts, sharp enough to burn
the skin, but Noah pressed forward, shoulders hunched, boots
breaking the crust with every step. He looked older now. He'd
grown taller and leaner. His hair grown long enough to curl from
under a frayed beanie. The weight of the pack bowed his frame,
straps biting into his shoulders, but he carried it without
complaint.

Moon padded close behind, ribs faint under her winter coat,
her once-white fur dulled to gray-brown with dirt. A child's
hoodie clung awkwardly around her torso, sleeves cut away, the
fabric torn but still clinging. Something scavenged and made hers.
She stayed at Noah's heels, head low, tail stiff, every movement
sharp with watchfulness.

Farther back, Mara dragged herself through the snow, a stick
gripped in one trembling hand, the other clutched tight to the
strap of her smaller pack. Her breath rattled with each exhale,

loud in the hush of snowfall, but she forced her pace steady. Every few steps she stumbled, caught herself, pushed on.

"Another storm's coming," she rasped, voice thin against the wind.

"I know," Noah said, eyes fixed ahead. "There should be shelter up here."

For a moment he slowed, glancing back at her. His face was shadowed by the beanie, older than it should've been. "Keep up, Mom."

She nodded, swallowing down another cough, and pushed her stick deeper into the snow. She looked at the age he'd gained in his face in the past few months. He needed someone to teach him how to shave already. It made her heart break.

No one spoke after that. The silence wasn't chosen. It was survival, the kind that made words too costly, too fragile to waste on the wind.

The drift broke beneath Noah's boots as they climbed the rise, snow giving way to the sagging silhouette ahead. The barn leaned against the wind, its roof bowed inward, shingles missing, half its frame swallowed in white. The walls groaned with every gust, but it stood. It was fragile and imperfect, but shelter none the less.

For a moment they all stopped. Not to celebrate, not even to rest, but to take in the fact that something still stood at all. A look passed between them. Thin relief, the kind born of necessity, not joy. For a moment, Mara thought he looked like a child again.

Noah shifted his pack higher on his shoulders, stepping forward first. Moon pressed close to his leg, ears pricked, body tense as if the snow itself might lunge. Mara lingered behind, her breath visible in quick clouds, leaning heavier on her stick.

The barn door was swollen with age, the wood gray and splintered. Noah put his shoulder into it, the hinges shrieking like something waking from a long sleep. The smell hit immediately. Rot, hay gone sour, dust thick enough to choke.

He held the door half-open, waiting. Every muscle coiled. The silence pressed in, broken only by the barn's ribs shifting in the wind.

Moon slipped through the gap, paws padding silent across the floorboards. She vanished into shadow, tail stiff.

Seconds dragged into minutes that felt like hours.

Then... the sharp rhythm of claws against wood, lighter, faster.

Moon burst back out, leaping into the snow with a sudden wag of her tail, tongue lolling. She barked once, almost playful.

Noah let his breath go, hand dropping from the strap of his pack. He glanced at Mara, then back into the dark maw of the barn.

"All clear," he muttered, pushing the door wider.

The barn swallowed them in damp silence. Dust motes hung in the weak shafts of light cutting through broken slats, drifting down onto mold-stained hay and the warped ribs of the floor. A cracked water barrel leaned against the far wall, half-frozen slush inside, and rusted farm tools lay scattered where they'd been left years ago. The place smelled of mildew, wood rot, and old animal musk... But it was four walls, and it was theirs.

"We can use some of these maybe," he mumbled as he looked over the old tools.

Noah dropped his pack with a dull thump, kneeling to unzip it. His hands moved steady, careful, like this was a ritual. One by one he laid their world out on the hay: two dented cans of beans, one already bulged at the side; a plastic bottle with less than a hand's worth of water left; a rag of jerky; a few matches wrapped in foil; the blanket already frayed from too much use. He set them down in neat rows, eyes flicking over each piece as if to memorize it. No wasted words. No unnecessary commentary. Just the numbers in his head, the math of survival.

Moon padded a slow circle of the barn, nose pressed to corners, claws clicking on warped boards. She sniffed at the tools, at the barrel, even at the hay, before trotting back to Noah. She sat with a soft huff, pressing her thin frame against his side, hoodie snagged and dirty. She didn't stray more than an arm's reach from him anymore.

"We'll have to melt snow for more water tonight," Mara looked at the stubble on his face when he spoke. She lowered herself onto the hay bale nearest the fire barrel, her stick clattering to the floor beside her. She rubbed her palms together, trying to draw warmth from the drafty air, her breath clouding faintly.

Then the cough hit. Sharp, ragged. She bent into her hand, shoulders shaking, the sound too raw to be just cold air.

Noah's head lifted immediately. His eyes tracked her, steady, unblinking.

"I'm fine," Mara said quickly, forcing a weak smile, swiping her mouth with her sleeve. "Just the cold. Nothing more."

Her voice wanted to sound casual, dismissive, but it frayed at the edges. She waved him off, reaching for the blanket he'd spread across the hay.

"I think I saw a drug store a few miles back. I'll go in the morning."

"No you won't. I'm fine." He knew she was lying.

Noah didn't answer. He just stared, silent, his jaw set. His eyes fell to the stick leaning against the wall, then back to the faint tremor in her hands.

He didn't argue. He didn't call her on it. He just watched her, the quiet pressing thick between them.

And in that silence, everything was understood: she was slipping. He knew it. She knew he knew it. Neither of them said a word.

The rusted barrel groaned when Noah shoved a few broken boards down into it. He struck a match, cupping it with both hands until the sputter caught, licking weakly along the splintered wood. Smoke curled thick and acrid at first, filling the barn with the stench of burning rot, but then the flame steadied, blooming into a wavering glow that pushed shadows back into the rafters.

They drew in close without speaking. Mara leaned toward the barrel, her knees tucked under the blanket, eyes hollow and glassy in the flicker. Her face looked sharper in the light. Her cheekbones carved thin, lips chapped. She wrapped her arms across her stomach like she was holding herself together.

Noah sat beside her, boots planted wide, his elbows braced on his knees. He kept feeding the fire small scraps, careful not to waste more than they could spare. Moon curled against his shin, ears twitching, nose resting across her paws. The hoodie on her back steamed faintly where snow had melted into the fabric.

The air inside the barn was still freezing. Every gust of wind shoved snow through the broken slats, scattering flurries across their faces, stinging cold against the heat of the flames. Tiny white flecks melted on Noah's beanie, on Mara's shoulders, dripping into the hay to vanish. The barn creaked with each shove of the storm, its bones protesting, but it held.

For a long time they sat in silence, just the pop of the fire and Mara's cough breaking the air.

Noah shifted finally, tugging the blanket higher over her shoulders. His hand lingered just a moment, steady, certain. His voice was clipped, deliberate, but carried no hesitation.

"We'll be okay, Ma."

Mara didn't look at him. She only stared into the barrel, watching the flames bend and crack, her breath rattling faintly with each exhale. She gave no answer.

The three of them huddled there in the glow, firelight flickering across tired faces, snow still slipping through the cracks above. For a moment, it almost looked like warmth could hold. A fragile island against the storm pressing at the walls. But the wind kept coming, and Mara's cough didn't stop.

Chapter IX

Evening settled fast, the sun swallowed behind low clouds, leaving the world blue and bruised. Noah crouched near the edge of the barn, the last scraps of daylight fading across the snow. His breath poured out in hard bursts as he jammed a rusty shovel into the frozen ground, hacking through the crust of ice until his gloves could claw the soil beneath.

He pulled up stringy roots, brittle and thin, snapping in his hands. Most crumbled to mush, but he stuffed them into his pocket anyway, every scrap a victory. Moon circled him tight, hoodie hanging askew on her bony frame. She froze whenever the wind shifted, ears pricking at phantoms in the distance, then pressed close again, as if tethered to his shadow.

By the time he went back inside, the light was almost gone. He stomped snow off his boots and set the roots on a cracked tin plate near the fire barrel. Mara stirred from where she was curled under blankets, her face pale in the glow.

"There's a drug store," Noah said. His voice was quiet, but firm. "In town. I saw it on the way here. I could make it in a day. Be back before dark tomorrow."

Her eyes sharpened despite the fever. "No."

"Moon would stay with you," he pressed, nodding toward the dog, who was already pressed close to Mara's side.

Her hand trembled as she pushed herself up on an elbow. "You go out there, you don't come back. You hear me? You don't come back." Her voice cracked, torn between fear and authority.

Noah's jaw set tight. He stared at the fire instead of answering.

Movement skittered at the edge of the barn. Noah froze, every nerve tight. A rat darted from a pile of rotted hay, its body fat for the season, whiskers twitching as it sniffed toward the roots he'd laid on the plate.

Noah's hand crept toward the pitchfork. He shifted slow, quiet, but the wood creaked beneath his boot. The rat bolted.

"Shit," he hissed, lunging after it.

Moon sprang, snapping teeth, but missed. The rat disappeared into a dark corner. Noah stalked it, breath sharp, the fork clutched like a spear. He waited, listened... the faint scuttle of claws on wood gave it away.

It burst along the wall, and he slammed the fork down. Missed again. Splinters flew where the tines gouged into the boards.

He chased it across the barn, heart hammering, Moon driving it back toward him with a snarl. Finally, it darted under a fallen beam.

A mistake.

Noah jammed the fork down hard, pinning the rat squealing against the floor. He leaned his whole weight on the handle, the sound twisting until it cut off sharp.

The rat squealed once before going still. Noah stood over it, chest heaving, pitchfork trembling in his hands. Moon panted beside him, tail twitching, eyes fixed on the prize.

He pulled the limp body free, blood streaking the wood.

"Yes! Meat!" He cheered. Mara watched him, the warmth from his face warmed her more than any fire could. She hadn't seen him smile since Christmas.

He carried it back to the fire like it was game worth boasting about. Mara looked up weakly from her place on the hay, lips parting as though to protest, but she closed them again when she saw his expression. Fierce, determined, older than his years.

Without a word, Noah set to work. He skinned the rat with stiff fingers, gutted it over a cracked tin plate. Then he dug out the last can of beans, scraped up the roots he'd scavenged from the snow, and melted handfuls of packed flakes into a battered pot.

The broth was thin, gray, and smelled more like smoke than food. He pinched in ashes from the bottom of the barrel as seasoning, crushing them between his fingers. He stirred it slow, watching the scraps bob.

When he ladled it out, Mara forced a smile. She took her portion without complaint, blowing across the surface, sipping like it was normal. Like it was gourmet soup, not rat and roots.

"Not as good as last year," Noah spoke between sips. "That sausage was something else, Mom."

"Yeah, It's good," she said softly. Her voice was too careful, but Noah let it stand.

He ate fast, hungry. Moon licked the last streaks from the bottom of her bowl, tail wagging weakly.

The night fell hard. Wind pressed through the slats, scattering flakes into the firelight. Mara sat propped against the wall, a tin cup in shaking hands. Water spilled down her chin as she drank, soaking her collar. Sweat gleamed on her forehead, even as her breath puffed white.

"It's fine," she rasped, wiping her mouth. "Just the cold."

Noah crouched near her, silent, watching. She coughed into her sleeve, trying to smother it, but it tore through anyway. He pulled the moldy hay closer to her side, spreading it like bedding even though the smell turned his stomach. She let him, too weak to argue.

He didn't speak again, not even when she tried to smile at him. She forced it, lips trembling, and then lurched forward, retching violently. Her thin shoulders heaved, the sound wet and raw, until nothing was left.

Noah caught her hair in his hand, held it back like he'd seen her do for Lena once, long ago. His other hand shook as he rubbed her back. He whispered nothing, because there was nothing to say.

When she slumped back, drained, he settled her against the wall, pulled the blanket higher. Her breathing rasped like saw teeth, uneven and ragged, filling the barn more than the firelight did.

Later, Noah lay on the cold hay, eyes open to the rafters. The barn creaked around him, every gust of wind pulling through the boards like a sigh. Moon pressed against his side, her body wiry but warm, the frayed hoodie bunched up under his chin.

The smell of vomit clung in the air, mixing with mold and smoke. He reached for the edge of the hoodie, tugged at the stretched fabric, and for a heartbeat he could see Lena last fall, grinning as she slipped it over her own head, laughing when the sleeves dangled too long. The sound of that laugh burned through him, bright and painful, before the silence rushed back in.

He pressed closer to Moon, his voice a whisper meant only for her. "We'll be okay."

But as the words left him, he knew they were thinner than before, worn down like everything else.

The barn settled heavy around them, less a shelter than a coffin waiting to be sealed.

Chapter X

Daylight seeped thin through the cracks in the barn walls, pale and weak, the kind of winter sun that gave no warmth. The fire in the barrel did little against it, a guttering glow swallowed by the shadows overhead. Smoke curled upward, staining the air. Snow hissed against the walls, drifting in through cracks, but inside it was all half-dark and silence.

Moon's head snapped up first. A low growl vibrated in her chest, deep enough that Noah froze mid-motion, hand hovering over the sticks he'd been feeding the fire. He held his breath and listened.

Then he heard it too... The crunch of boots in snow outside, steady, heavy, pausing, then coming closer.

Mara stirred on the hay, propping herself up with effort. Her voice was a rasp, barely air.

"Stay quiet."

The steps stopped. For a moment, nothing. Just the barn creaking and Noah's heart hammering in his ears. He prepared himself for a fight, eyes darting for a weapon.

It only sounded like one, but even one slimbie could be a challenge.

Then a voice called in, muffled through the wood. Too bright, almost cheerful, the kind of cheer that came from memory instead of truth.

"Hello? Anyone in there? Don't mean no harm. Just lookin' for somewhere to warm up."

Moon's growl deepened, her body low, hackles stiff. Noah's hand slid to the pitchfork propped near the barrel, fingers wrapping the smoothed wood. He didn't answer. He wasn't sure what was better.

A slimbie, or a stranger.

The voice tried again.

"Cold'll kill a man faster than hunger. I ain't here to take nothin'. Promise!"

A long silence. Then the barn door groaned, wood and ice grinding, until it gave way with a sudden wrench.

Daylight speared into the dark. The dim light felt blinding to their unadjusted eyes. A rush of cold air followed, biting their faces, snow spilling across the floorboards. The firelight shrank back against the blaze of white, and in the gap stood a man.

He was lean, eyes wide in a too-thin face, beard crusted with frost. Layers of scavenged clothes hung crooked on him: torn flannel, a jacket ripped at the arm, a scarf that looked like an old towel. He lifted his hands high, palms empty, fingers raw and cracked from the cold.

"See?" he said, showing them to the light like it was proof. "No trouble. Just cold."

Noah didn't lower the fork. He planted himself between Mara and the door. The fire warmed one side of his face, the outside glare froze the other.

Moon stood taut and silent, throat thrumming. The man's smile flickered, then returned, thin as the wind behind him.

The man shifted his satchel, crouching just inside the door so the light fell across him. With his cracked fingers he fished out a strip of something dark, stiff. Jerky. It looked tough as leather, edges whitish with salt.

"See?" he said, voice low but steady. "I got food. Nothin' fancy, but it keeps you alive."

He tore off a piece with his teeth, chewed like it took work. Then he tossed a scrap toward the ground between them.

Moon's growl thickened as she sniffed, claws skidding faintly on the packed dirt. She leaned forward, muscles bunched.

"No," Noah said sharply. His voice cut the space. "Stay."

Her ears flicked back. She froze, eyes locked on the scrap. The man's smile quivered.

"Dog knows better than most folks I meet," he muttered, and bit again into his own strip, exaggerating the chew. "It's safe enough. Just don't ask what animal it is."

He held another small shred out between two fingers, almost an offering. "Won't hurt her. Or you."

Noah's grip flexed on the pitchfork, then slowly eased. He stepped forward, snatched the strip, and bit down hard. It was dry, stringy, salt scratching the back of his throat. He forced himself to chew, forced his face not to twist.

Moon waited only a beat before she lunged for the scrap on the floor, jaws snapping it up. She gnawed fast, tail low, then licked the dirt clean where it had fallen.

Noah let out a thin breath. The pitch fork dipped a fraction. His shoulders lowered.

From the corner of the firelight, Mara watched. Her face was half-shadow, the scarf pulled tight around her neck. She coughed once into her sleeve, eyes narrowing, but said nothing.

The man's smile settled easier now. "See? Nothin' bad," he said. "I told you. Just tryin' to stay alive same as you."

They ended up circling the barrel fire, each keeping a careful wedge of space between. The stranger squatted low, arms loose over his knees, the heat making his beard drip faintly with melt.

He spoke easily, words spilling like he'd been waiting a long time to hear his own voice bounce off walls again.

Hours passed as he told tale after tale.

Names of towns, of people, of roads... All of it interesting.

But none of it lined up.

One moment he'd been working a rig downstate, the next he swore he'd walked all the way from Ohio. His stories folded over themselves, changed detail mid-sentence. He laughed at things only he seemed to hear.

Moon never settled. She paced slow circles near Noah, hackles faintly raised, eyes never leaving the man. Every creak of his satchel, every scrape of his boots, she was there. Her weight forward, low growl flickering in her throat.

Mara sat on the hay with her shoulders hunched, a blanket pulled up around her neck. Her body always angled, always making a wall between Noah and the man. Even when she coughed, doubling over into her sleeve, her hand would come down after, steady, placed lightly on Noah's wrist like an anchor.

Noah's eyes kept drifting to the stranger's pockets. Lumpy bulges, crinkled wrappers. The sound of something rattling when he shifted. Food. More than he'd shown. Noah didn't say it, but his stomach twisted with the knowing.

The man caught his stare once and smirked. He dug into his coat, pulled out a battered flask with the cap hanging by a strip of tape. He swirled it, liquid sloshing inside. "Whiskey," he said, tilting it toward Noah like an offering. "Good for the blood in this kind of cold. Warm you right through."

Noah's fingers tightened on his knees. He shook his head. "No. I'm too young."

The man chuckled, the sound low and raw. "Look man enough to me."

Before Noah could answer, Mara's voice cut in, weak but sharp as a snapped twig. "He said he's too young."

The man's smile twitched, hung there. "Alright, ma'am. Didn't mean nothin' by it."

Mara coughed then, sudden and tearing, her whole body folding in on itself. The blanket slipped down her shoulder, bones too sharp under her shirt. Noah was at her side instantly, lifting the blanket back, hand braced at her back until the cough passed.

Moon pressed in close, whining, nose brushing Mara's knee.

The barn groaned with the night wind. Snow hissed through the gaps. The stranger leaned back against the wall, shadows painting across his face, his flask hanging loose in one hand. His eyes stayed on them too long before finally sliding away.

Noah pulled the blanket tighter around his mother. She leaned into him, exhausted, her breath shallow. They didn't speak again. Just the crackle of the barrel fire, Moon's soft pacing, and the stranger's slow, steady sipping while they drifted down toward uneasy sleep.

Chapter XI

Noah jerked awake to a sound he knew too well. Moon's growl, low and steady, like a wire pulled tight. The fire in the barrel had gone down to coals, orange shadows licking across the barn's ribs. The air was thick with smoke and cold.

Moon stood stiff at the foot of Mara's make shift bedding, her teeth bared, eyes fixed on the dark shape leaning over her.

The stranger.

His hand hovered above Mara's throat, fingers spread like claws. His breath steamed in the air, sour with whiskey and old hunger. His eyes flicked toward Noah, and the cheer he'd worn earlier was gone, peeled back to something gaunt and feral.

"Stay down, boy," he whispered, voice cracked raw. "This ain't your world anymore."

Noah's hand fumbled for the pitchfork, clumsy with sleep and fear. His heart pounded so loud he thought the man must hear it. His legs shook as he got to his feet, the wood rough against his palms.

"You need to leave," Noah said. His voice surprised him... it didn't break. It sounded deeper than it had before. Like he had suddenly become a man in that very moment.

The stranger laughed, dry and bitter. "You think you can tell me? Little pup like you?" He crouched lower over Mara. "She don't got long anyhow. Better I make use of what's left."

"No."

"Oh come on, boy! You probably ain't had nothing yet to know what you're missing... How about I give you some more of that jerky?"

He reached slowly into his pocket...

Moon snapped, lunging forward a half-step. The man kicked out, catching her in the ribs, sending her yelping back. Noah moved at the same time, thrusting the pitchfork forward. The stranger twisted, and the tines only raked his jacket, tearing the fabric.

The man's hand shot out, fast, gripping the fork's handle. His strength jolted Noah. He yanked hard, and the fork almost slipped from Noah's grip. The older man sneered, leaning into him, breath hot and rancid.

"You're just a kid," he spat, forcing Noah backward, inch by inch. "A stupid kid with a stupid dog!"

The pitchfork shuddered between them, the stranger's weight pressing it down toward the floor. Noah's knees buckled, his arms screamed. He couldn't hold him.

Moon launched again, this time clamping her teeth around the man's hand. The stranger roared, blood spraying across the hay as she tore into him. His grip faltered, just enough.

Noah shoved forward with everything he had left. The fork slammed into the man's side with a wet crunch. The stranger howled, staggering, but still on his feet. His fist lashed out, catching Noah across the cheek. White light exploded behind Noah's eyes. He reeled, almost dropping the fork.

"Not enough!" the man snarled, staggering toward him, blood running down his hip, his hand shredded by Moon's jaws. "Come on back, boy!"

Noah's chest heaved. He set his feet. He drove the fork in again, this time lower, harder. The tines sank deep, and the man's scream turned into a gurgle. He swung one last time, weak, missing Noah's head by inches.

Noah yanked the fork out and stabbed again. And again. Hot blood hissed in the cold air, spattering the boards. The stranger sagged, knees buckling, then went down hard, the weight of him shaking the floor.

Noah stood over him, shoulders heaving, the fork shaking in his hands. Moon growled low, lips wet with blood, standing guard as the man twitched once, then lay still.

He held the forks over the mans head for a moment, waiting for him to turn.

Seconds turned to minutes.

Then the stranger's eyes flickered, and Noah shoved the forks through his eyes.

The barn went quiet. The only sound left was Noah's ragged breath, Moon's panting, and the soft rattle of Mara's cough in the dark.

"Noah..." Mara's voice was thin, hoarse. Her eyes glimmered in the firelight. She'd seen it all.

He didn't answer. Couldn't. He just stared at the body at his feet, the steam rising off it, the blood already turning black on the frozen floor.

"Noah," Mara's voice cracked, weak but urgent. She lay propped on one elbow, her lips pale, eyes hollow but steady. She lifted a trembling hand toward him. "Come here."

He stepped over the dead man without looking down, knees wobbling but refusing to bend. He lowered himself beside her, the pitchfork clutched like a cane.

Her fingers brushed his wrist. They were hot with fever, paper-thin. "You saved us," she whispered. "You're strong. Stronger than I ever was."

Noah stared at the fire, not her. His voice came out flat, scraped raw. "I killed him."

"You had to."

"He was stronger than me. If Moon hadn't..." His throat caught. He swallowed hard. His eyes welled. "I almost lost."

Mara's eyes watered, though not from the sickness this time. "But you didn't. You did what you had to do."

Noah shook his head slowly. His face stayed blank, but his words trembled. "It doesn't matter. He's gone now. Just like the others." He drew a shaky breath. "Everyone goes." He reached up, wiping the tears from his eyes.

Her grip tightened on him, frail but desperate. "Don't say that."

"It's true." He finally looked at her, eyes hollow, cheeks blotched red from the cold. "First Dad. Then Lena. Now this one. You'll be next. Then me."

The words dropped between them like stones. Mara's face twisted, but she didn't argue. She only pulled her hand back to her chest, coughing into it until blood flecked her sleeve. She had been a good mother. At least, she thought she had. This wasn't the little boy she'd raised. Not anymore.

Noah sat there a long time, staring at the barrel's fading flame. Moon curled tighter against his hip, as if anchoring him. His knuckles stayed locked on the pitchfork until they ached.

Later, he dragged the man's body outside. He didn't bury it. He just left it laying next to the barn. The snow took it quickly, wind blowing over it, drifts building across the slack face and twisted limbs. In minutes, it was half-buried, the world already erasing what had happened.

Noah stood at the threshold, the door cracked open, the cold biting at his face. He didn't look back.

Chapter XII

Daylight tried to squeeze through the walls, washed gray and sickly as if even the sky was tired of the season. The fire in the barrel had burned down to a dull glow, more smoke than warmth. Noah had run out of scrap wood lying around the barn. Every corner of the barn felt damp with cold.

Mara lay flat on the hay, her body sinking deeper each day into its rough cushion. Sweat glazed her forehead despite the chill, strands of hair plastered to her cheeks. Her breaths came shallow and uneven, rattling in her chest like loose nails in a tin can.

Noah crouched beside her with a tin cup, dipping the spoon carefully into the melted snow inside. He steadied her head with one hand, coaxed the spoon to her lips with the other. "Slow," he murmured. His voice had gone flat in the days since the stranger. Like it had been stripped of its edges.

Mara sipped weakly, most of it running down her chin. She coughed, wet and sharp, and pushed his hand away. "Enough," she rasped.

"You need it," Noah said, but he didn't try again. He set the cup down by her side, close enough for when she could manage it. His hands stayed on his knees a moment longer, knuckles pale in the half-light.

Her eyes found his, cloudy and tired but still searching. "I'm slowing you down," she whispered, voice breaking around the words.

Noah shook his head, quick, almost defensive. "No."

"I am." A faint smile touched her lips, bitter and resigned. "Always have been."

He looked away, fingers brushing at Moon's fur where she'd pressed in close. The dog whined low in her throat, head resting near Mara's shoulder, eyes sharp on every sound.

"You're wrong," Noah said at last. He kept his voice low, even. "We're still here. That's because of you."

Mara's hand trembled as she reached for him. He caught it before it could fall back to her chest, held it tight enough to steady the shaking. For a moment she closed her eyes, letting her breath move through the cage of her ribs, ragged and fragile, as the barn groaned in the cold around them.

Noah stayed crouched by her side, her hand in his, as if that single tether could keep her anchored. Her skin felt damp and too warm, her pulse fluttering like a trapped bird beneath paper-thin flesh.

Her eyes opened again, glassy and rimmed red, but they fixed on him with a clarity that pierced through the fever. "Noah," she whispered, her voice worn thin as thread.

"I'm here," he said quickly, leaning close.

Her lips trembled with the shape of a smile, though it never quite formed. She swallowed, every movement stiff with effort. "You're stronger than I ever was. Stronger than I thought you'd have to be." A weak, broken laugh escaped, immediately overtaken by a cough that bent her frame and shook her shoulders.

"Don't," Noah said, as if the word could shield her.

But she kept going, eyes shining with fever and something deeper. "The world's cruel for making you grow up like this. Cruel for stealing the boy from you so fast. But..." She sucked in a shallow breath, let it rattle out. "Don't let it take the rest. Don't... be afraid of it. Don't hide. Survive it. That's all that matters now."

Noah's jaw tightened. His face looked hollow in the firelight, cast in hard planes that didn't belong on a boy. He wanted to argue, to beg her to stop talking like she was already gone, but the words stuck like stones in his throat.

She squeezed his hand, the smallest pressure, barely felt. "I'm sorry," she whispered. Her gaze blurred, then found him again, swimming with regret. "For everything I couldn't give you. For everything I couldn't stop."

His breath shuddered in and out, but when he spoke his voice stayed steady, flat with a kind of weary finality. "It's okay."

"I love you, Noah," the words were weak on her breath.

The silence that followed seemed endless, filled only by the wind clawing at the barn. She closed her eyes for a moment, lashes trembling, then forced them open again to keep him in her sight.

Noah leaned down until his forehead almost touched hers. His voice was a whisper only she could hear. "Merry Christmas, Mom."

Her lips curved at last, faint and fragile. For one flicker of a second, she looked peaceful. Then her chest seized, arching her body, the sound of her breath breaking into a ragged, tearing rattle. It dragged on, faltered, and at last, slipped out of her like a candle blown bare.

Her head sagged against the hay. The faint smile lingered, frozen in place.

Noah didn't let go of her hand. He sat there in the half-dark, Moon pressed so tight against his leg he could feel the dog trembling. The fire guttered low, throwing shadows that seemed to lean closer, as though the barn itself were bowing into grief.

He stayed like that until the stillness settled heavy and permanent across the room.

For a long time Noah didn't move. His hand stayed locked around hers, the skin cooling under his palm, her fingers slack now in a way that made his stomach twist. The silence pressed in thick, broken only by the faint crackle of dying fire. Moon shifted restlessly, whining low in her throat, her body rigid against Noah's leg.

Then it happened.

A twitch. At first so small he thought it was in him, not her. Mara's hand shivered against his, just once, then again, jerky and unnatural. Her chest, still minutes ago, hitched with a hollow gasp.

Noah's head snapped up. "Mom?"

Her eyes opened. They were clouded, glass filmed over in milky gray, no recognition in them, no warmth. Her lips peeled back, not in a smile this time but a snarl, guttural and wet. Her whole body jolted forward like a puppet pulled by the strings.

"No!"

She lunged at him, the sound tearing from her throat an animal rasp. Her teeth clacked shut where his shoulder had been a heartbeat before. Noah fell back into the hay, scrambling, heart slamming against his ribs.

Moon exploded into motion, teeth flashing as she tried to wedge herself between them. But Mara's body thrashed with sudden, monstrous strength, sending hay flying as she reached again for her son.

Noah's hand found the pitchfork. He ripped it up between them, the wood slick in his grip. His face was blank now. No fear.

No tears. Just a hollow, practiced focus that didn't belong to a boy his age.

"I'm sorry," he said, voice flat.

Then he drove the fork into her head.

The sound was thick, wet, a crack of bone under metal. She jerked once, hands clawing at the handle, then stilled. Her mouth gaped, one last shudder rolling through her body, and then her body went limp, head pinned to the wall.

Noah stayed crouched over her, both hands locked on the fork, chest heaving. The barn was dead quiet again, except for Moon's panting. The dog pressed against him, whimpering softly, her muzzle streaked with straw.

Noah let out a long, shaky breath and pulled the fork free. Her body slumped to the floor, completely still. He stared down at the ruin in the hay, expression stripped clean of childhood, of softness, of anything left to give. His shoulders sagged, but he didn't cry.

The fire in the barrel hissed as a log broke and crumbled inward. Its glow caught his face, sharp and hollow, eyes fixed on nothing.

"Goodbye, Mom," he whispered, but there was no tremor in it, no break. Just words falling flat into the cold air. "I love you."

Moon pressed closer, her body trembling. Noah rested a hand on her head, the motion slow, mechanical, as if it was the only thing keeping him from unraveling.

Outside, the wind carried snow against the barn door, piling in drifts that would cover everything soon enough.

Noah's hands were raw before he even began, the shovel blade clanging useless against earth gone iron under the snow. He tried anyway, gouging shallow scrapes, pushing until the wood handle bit into his palms. Moon paced beside him, whining, but he didn't stop. He couldn't.

Every few minutes he looked back at the barn door. Her body lay there, wrapped in the only blanket they had worth anything, hair spilling out across the edge, stiff now, face hidden. She looked small in the bundle. Too small.

The snow fell harder. It filled the pit he was carving before it could even hold depth. He knew it wasn't enough, knew the ground would give her back in spring, but he kept digging until his arms shook and his breath burned white out of him.

When the hole was no deeper than his knees, he stopped. He stood there, chest heaving, shovel dangling loose at his side. Then he went back for her.

He didn't think as he lifted her, he just did it. Bracing the bundle against his shoulder, legs straining under the weight. She was lighter than she should've been. He hated that thought, and shoved it away.

Moon followed, silent now, ears flat.

He lowered Mara into the shallow grave, blanket and all. Snow dusted her face where the cloth slipped, clinging to her lashes, painting her pale and still. For a moment he just stared, shovel still clutched in one hand like a farmer who'd forgotten to put down his tool.

"I'll take it from here," he said softly. The words came out flat, not promise, not prayer. Just a line in the snow between then and now.

He filled the grave with quick, violent shovels, not caring how clumsy it looked. Each scrape and thud rang louder than it should've in the white silence. The snow swallowed sound, swallowed her, swallowed him.

When it was done, the mound was crooked, uneven. He didn't fix it. He just stood there, shovel buried in the drift, watching his breath rise like smoke over the spot where his mother lay.

Moon pressed against his leg. He didn't bend to touch her.

No tears came. Not one. His face was carved blank, the wind burning it red, his eyes dry and hard. Somewhere deep, something had cracked and gone out, and there was no getting it back.

The snow kept falling. Already it softened the mound, covering it smooth, erasing her.

Noah turned and walked back toward the barn without looking over his shoulder. Moon padded after him.

Behind them, the world closed up again, white on white, as if she had never been there at all.

Part 4

Chapter XIII

The road cut through the snow like an old scar, cracked asphalt showing through in patches where the wind had scraped it clean. Noah moved down the center of it, shoulders squared, the weight of his pack pulling him into a steady, deliberate rhythm.

He looked older than his years now. Another head taller, broad-shouldered, a beard thick across his jaw. His face was harder, sharper, carved into angles by cold and hunger. The boy was gone. What walked here was something leaner, built from loss and survival.

The axe in his hand was worn smooth at the haft, the head dulled but still lethal. Every step he took was measured. His eyes never stopped moving. Edges of buildings, drifted cars, the black mouths of alleys. The world had taught him to see threat in every shadow.

Moon padded at his heel, larger now, no softness left in her frame. Scars ridged the fur along her shoulder. She carried herself with the taut silence of a hunter, her ribs showing faint under her wiry off-white coat. She looked more wolf than dog, ears pricked, eyes flashing at every shift of wind. The ragged hoodie hanging on by threads fluttered against the snow-light, the last trace of color in a dead world.

Neither made a sound beyond boots crunching crust and claws clicking faintly on ice. Not desperate survivors anymore. Predators. Partners.

They crested a low rise and the church came into view. The steeple leaned crooked, its bell tower split open by storms, glass long since blown from the windows. Snow had drifted through the empty arches, blanketing the roof and piling against the sagging doors.

Noah slowed. His grip shifted on the axe. He scanned the angles, every corner, every line of broken wall. Then he motioned once, low. Moon froze, her body rigid, nose lifting toward the wind.

The front doors were swollen and warped, but one hung loose enough to be tested. Noah pressed his shoulder against it and let Moon slip inside, eyes narrowing as dim light cut through fractured stained glass.

Seconds drew out. A minute passed. A single bark from inside the door let him know it was safe.

The place smelled of mold and rot. Pews lay splintered and collapsed, some shoved sideways as if by panicked crowds years ago. The altar was bare stone now, draped in dust. Colored shards from the windows scattered across the floor, catching what little sun pushed through the clouds outside.

Noah moved slow, methodical. He checked the aisles, the corners, the pulpit. Moon slunk ahead, nose brushing the ground, claws scratching wood as she traced her path. They made one full sweep before Noah let his shoulders ease a fraction.

They found a back room with a broken door hanging half off its hinges. An office once, maybe. The shelves had collapsed, papers rotted to mush, but the walls closed in tighter than the vast hollow of the sanctuary. Easier to defend.

Noah dropped his pack and pulled out what scraps remained: half a tin of beans, a twist of dried meat, the blanket they shared. He struck a small fire from broken chair legs, coaxing it in the dented barrel he'd dragged against the wall. Smoke curled upward, seeping through the cracks in the ceiling.

Moon circled once, twice, before dropping at his feet, curling tight into herself with a sigh. Her eyes stayed open, though, bright and watchful.

Noah sat against the wall, axe resting across his knees. Firelight flickered across his face, deepening the hollows under his eyes, sharpening the line of his beard. He looked older than any sixteen-year-old should have a right to. Older, and harder.

The church creaked around them, wind threading through broken windows, snow whispering against the walls. For now, it was shelter. For now, it was enough.

Dawn pushed through what was left of the ruined glass in pale strips of color, staining the dust and snow with dull reds and blues. The fire had long since guttered out, leaving only the sharp bite of cold and the faint smell of ash in the room.

Noah stirred against the wall, joints stiff, back aching from the stone floor beneath the thin blanket. He pulled on his jacket, movements slow, mechanical, the weariness of survival pressed into every bone.

Moon uncurled beside him with a grunt, stretching long, claws scraping wood. She shook frost from her coat and padded to the doorway, ears pricked.

Noah slung his pack over one shoulder, took up the axe. He moved toward the main hall, eyes narrowed against the sting of cold air seeping through the cracks.

Then he stopped.

The silence was wrong. Too heavy, too present. Not empty, but waiting.

He stepped through the doorway into the sanctuary, boots whispering against snow drifted across the stone floor.

Shapes filled the pews.

At first his mind refused it... Shadows, maybe, or tricks of the light. But they shifted, heads twitching, fingers drumming against wood. Dozens of them. Hollow-eyed, skin stretched thin, jaws slack.

Slimbies.

They weren't rushing him. Not yet. Didn't even notice him.

Some sat in the pews as if still listening to sermons that would never come. Some knelt with hands clasped, swaying faintly, their mouths working around soundless prayers. One rocked in the corner, forehead thudding again and again against the stone.

It was mimicry. Grotesque, instinctive echoes of lives they no longer had. A congregation of hunger worshiping nothing.

Noah froze mid-step, axe tight in his hand. His breath caught hard in his chest.

The air in the church felt too thick to breathe. Dust floated in the colored shafts of dawn, drifting like incense above the rows of ruined pews. The Slimbies didn't move all at once, just little twitches, shoulders jerking, fingers tapping wood, jaws grinding slow as if remembering the rhythm of prayer.

Noah stood locked in place, heart hammering, every muscle screaming at him to move but afraid that the smallest sound would set them off.

Moon's growl deepened, low and dangerous, vibrating through the quiet like a warning bell. A dozen heads turned toward it in unison, necks creaking as if pulled by the same invisible string. Their eyes caught the light, pale and empty, but fixed with terrible hunger.

Noah shifted his weight back, step by step toward the door. The silence stretched thin, a wire ready to snap.

Then it did.

Something small slammed against his leg. He looked down...

A child. Skin gray and splitting at the seams, arms too thin to be whole. Its teeth sank through the fabric of his pants into the meat of his calf.

The sound tore out of him raw, half shout, half gasp. Pain flared hot as fire. He kicked hard, the body rag-dolling loose but clinging with its teeth until they tore free, leaving blood slick down his boot.

The noise shattered the stillness.

Every Slimbie in the pews turned at once. Heads jerked. Backs arched. A low moan rippled through the sanctuary, rising into a chorus as dozens of bodies pushed upright, pews creaking, splintering under their weight.

The congregation had risen.

The pews cracked under the sudden lurch of bodies. A wave of them surged forward, arms clawing, teeth gnashing, hunger spilling into the air like rot.

Noah roared and swung. The axe came down through a skull, splitting bone and sending black spittle across the altar stones. He ripped it free, pivoted, buried it in another chest. The wood handle bucked in his hands, but his grip was iron.

They kept coming. He didn't back away. He drove into them.

One lunged from the side, Noah's boot slammed into its ribs, snapping them like twigs. Another clambered over a pew.

He swung low, severing its legs, then crushed its head under his heel.

Moon was a blur at his flank, jaws tearing throats, fur flashing as she snapped and ripped. Blood smeared the hoodie at her neck.

The swarm pressed closer. Arms wrapped around Noah's shoulders, clawing for his face. He shoved forward, bellowing, muscles straining as he tore free and brought the axe down again, again, again. His beard and chest were soaked red now, his breath ragged, his face lit wild with fury.

They dragged at him from every side. He fought like a tank rolling into fire, unbreakable, unstoppable, even as teeth sank into his arm, his shoulder, his back. He didn't cry out. He answered with steel, with boots, with fists.

Moon leapt onto a Slimbie's back, tearing its ear away in a spray of blood, but another hand clamped around her midsection. The hoodie she wore, ragged and faded, a ruined memory of Lena, tore as the creature ripped at it. She thrashed free, cloth hanging in ribbons, the last shred of her comfort ripped to pieces.

She landed hard, teeth bared, but froze when she saw him.

Noah was going under.

The axe slipped from his grip as arms pinned his shoulders, his chest, his legs. Dozens of teeth sank into him at once. He vanished beneath a mass of bodies, his voice still tearing out. Raw, guttural, unyielding... until it broke into screams.

Until the screams broke into silence.

Moon stood at the front of the church, chest heaving, torn hoodie hanging from her shoulders in strips. She whimpered once, high and sharp, a sound that cut through the feeding frenzy.

Every head turned.

Her ears pinned back. She bolted, claws scrabbling across stone, shoving through the half-hung door into the snow.

The last thing she saw when she looked back was the swarm still moving over him, a tide of hunger swallowing her boy whole.

She ran.

Snow swallowed the sound as soon as Moon broke into the open air. The cold hit her like knives, but she didn't stop. Her paws tore through drifts, claws biting ice, the breath ripping from her throat in sharp clouds.

Behind her, the church groaned in its bones. From inside came the muffled chorus of feeding. The low, wet rasp of teeth on flesh, the cracking of pews under the crush of bodies. His screams were gone now, swallowed whole by the swarm.

Moon stumbled once, caught herself, kept running. Lena's hoodie, what was left of it, flapped uselessly from her neck. Torn to ribbons, trailing her like a shadow.

She reached the road and skidded to a halt, sides heaving, ears twitching toward the soundless gray horizon. The world looked empty, blank, as if nothing had ever lived in it at all.

She whined, sharp and thin, head low, tail tucked. Her eyes flicked back to the broken doors of the church. The dark inside shifted faintly, a body rising, another, more turning toward the gap.

She didn't wait.

Moon bolted down the road, her small shape swallowed quick by the storm. Snow fell harder, layering over her pawprints, erasing them step by step until there was nothing left but white.

Behind her, the church sagged silent again, its congregation still kneeling, still feeding, as if worship had simply taken another form.

Chapter XIV

Snow layered the city in silence, the streets swallowed by white drifts that turned every ruin into the same shape. Cars sagged beneath it, windows frosted blind. Doors stood frozen shut, their hinges crusted in ice.

Moon padded through it alone.

Her paws sank deep, leaving a trail behind her that the wind began erasing before she'd gone ten steps. Her ribs showed sharp under her wiry coat, every movement lean with hunger. The hoodie she'd worn had completely deteriorated away, leaving only the ragged pink collar with a single tag around her neck.

She nosed through an overturned trash bin, teeth clinking against a frozen can. Nothing inside but a smear of rot she couldn't swallow. She kept moving.

The air smelled wrong everywhere. Mildew, rust, the faint sour tang of Slimbies moving somewhere out of sight. She stayed low to the ground, head swinging side to side, ears sharp for the scrape of feet or the rasp of breath.

An old diner loomed at the corner, its windows busted out, stools still standing in a row at the counter. Moon slipped through the gap, claws ticking against tile, and sniffed at the corners. Grease long since turned to mold. She found a rat frozen stiff near the back door and cracked it between her teeth. The crunch echoed through the hollow place, louder than it should have.

She froze, muzzle streaked red, ears pricked.

Nothing. Only the wind whining through the empty booths.

She dragged the rat carcass to the counter, swallowed it whole, and licked her teeth clean. The taste lingered bitter, but it was enough to keep her moving.

Outside again, the city yawned endless and white, the horizon blurred by blowing snow. No voices. No footsteps. Just her, the silence, and the ghosts that lived in it.

Moon pressed on.

She found them in the open lot of a collapsed market.

At first, she thought they were Slimbies. Thin, jerking movements, clothes shredded and filthy. But then one lifted his head, and she saw the eyes: alive, sunken deep in a starving face.

There were four of them. Men, maybe once strong, now little more than bone and sinew stretched tight. They crouched around a barrel that held no fire, only smoke rising from something charred at the bottom.

One of them saw her. His mouth opened, not in a moan, but a grin that showed teeth black with rot.

"Meat," he croaked.

The others turned.

"Go slow. Don't scare it off."

Moon's hackles rose, lips curling, but her paws froze. The smell rolled off them. Sweat, hunger, sickness. Worse than Slimbies. Worse because they still knew what they wanted.

They spread out, slow and careful, arms open like they were welcoming her. "Easy, dog," one whispered, his voice cracked but coaxing. Another licked his lips.

"Come on over here, girl..."

A loop of rope swung from the hand of the third.

Moon bolted.

She hit the weeds at the lot's edge, but something whistled past and snapped tight around her back legs. The rope yanked hard, flipping her onto her side. The ground slammed her ribs, breath knocked out. She thrashed, claws tearing dirt, teeth flashing as she snapped at the cord.

"Hold her!" one of them shouted, voice breaking with excitement. "Hold her!"

Hands grabbed at her fur, pressing down, fingers clawing for her throat. She twisted and sank her teeth deep into a wrist. The man screamed, hot blood spraying across her muzzle. The others swarmed closer, but she tore free with a surge of panic, rope slipping loose in her frenzy.

She ripped away from them, her paws tearing through weeds, her ears full of their shouts. Rocks clattered behind her, someone giving chase for a dozen staggering steps before collapsing in the dirt.

Moon didn't stop running until the lot was a smear behind her and the only sound left was her own panting.

She didn't look back.

The thaw came sudden, like the world had broken open overnight. Snow melted into rivers that cut through the streets, water rushing black with oil and ash. The cars that had been buried all winter reappeared half-submerged, their metal skins rusting through in the flood.

Moon waded belly-deep across what had been an intersection, the current tugging at her legs. Her fur clung dark and heavy, every step a fight. She shook water from her ears and scrambled onto the hood of a car, panting steam into the damp air.

The city stank now. Everything rotting at once. Meat, mold, gas, all stirred into one choking breath. She gagged against it, nose twitching as she searched for what could still be eaten.

She found it in an alley, half hidden in the weeds that had already begun pushing through the cracks. A nest of rats, slick and blind, squealed under the rubble. She lunged, teeth flashing, and came up with three writhing bodies clamped in her jaws. Their blood spilled hot across her tongue.

The sound carried.

From the end of the alley came a shuffle. Then another.

She froze, lips curled back, tail stiff.

Figures swayed into view. Four of them, clothes plastered to their frames from the flood, skin sloughing in the wet. Their mouths opened in unison, the sound that came out not quite moan, not quite breath, but a hollow rasp that filled the narrow space.

Moon backed away, rat carcasses hanging limp from her jaws. When the first one reached, she spun and darted beneath a wrecked sedan half-sunk in the street. Their feet slapped water as they followed, arms raking across the metal, fingers clawing for her fur.

She pressed flat to the ground, belly scraping wet pavement, heart hammering. The Slimbies clawed and rasped above her, their gray hands tearing strips of rust free, but they couldn't reach her. Their heads banged against the car frame as they lurched and shoved, blind with hunger.

Moon didn't move. Not until their groans faded, steps dragging them farther down the alley.

Only then did she slip free, soaked and trembling, and vanish into the drowned streets.

The heat of summer came heavy and endless. Sun glared off the broken windows and turned the streets into ovens, baking the stink of rot into the air until it hung like a weight.

Moon panted with her tongue lolling, each breath shallow, her ribs working like bellows under her coat. The collar that once clung to her neck was faded, barely more than a scrap now. All she had left were scars and a coat patchy from hunger.

She found shade beneath the skeleton of a bus tipped onto its side. The metal burned against her fur as she squeezed through a gap and collapsed inside. The air smelled of rubber and dust, the seats long since melted to skeleton frames.

Her head sank against her paws. The world swam.

In the haze of heat, memory pressed close. Not words, not thoughts. Just shapes. A boy's hand, rough with calluses, resting against her head. A woman's laugh that vibrated warm in her chest. The tug of a hoodie being pulled over her head.

She whined in her sleep.

When her eyes snapped open again, the images were gone. The bus was silent, only the cicadas shrilling outside. Her throat burned with thirst. She dragged herself up, legs stiff, and forced her way back into the white glare.

The road wavered in the heat, stretched thin like a mirage. She pressed on, step after step, moving only because stopping meant never moving again.

By autumn the city had changed again.

The heat broke, and with it came wind that rattled through the hollow buildings, scattering leaves across the cracked asphalt. Vines choked the walls of old storefronts, branches bent heavy with seedpods, weeds tall enough to hide rusting cars to their mirrors.

Moon moved through it like a ghost. Her frame was leaner now, wiry muscle drawn over bone, her coat thickened again against the cold. Scars mapped her muzzle and shoulders where teeth had found her, narrow pink lines that never grew hair back.

She slipped between shadows, no longer the pup that barked and bounded at Noah's side. She had learned the quiet ways: wait, watch, move only when the wind moved too.

At the corner of an intersection, she stopped.

A Slimbie stood in the center of the street, arms hanging loose, head sagging like it had forgotten the weight of itself. Its jaw worked in little spasms, chewing on nothing.

Moon crouched low, body still, eyes locked on its swaying form. When the wind shifted, carrying her scent, its head twitched. Its empty eyes snapped wide, searching.

She was already gone.

The weeds swallowed her as she darted through, paws quick and sure. She knew the dance now: slip past, never challenge, vanish before hunger found her.

By the time she reached the far block, the Slimbie was nothing but a shadow behind her.

She stopped again, sides heaving, nose lifted to the air.

The wind carried something new. Not rot. Not rust. Not carrion.

She whined low in her throat, then pushed forward, nose to the wind.

The city stretched ahead, choked with weeds and shadows, but for the first time in a year, she was not just moving. She was following.

Chapter XV

The wind shifted.

Her head snapped up, nose twitching, ears pricked. Not rot. Not rust. Not carrion. Something else.

It threaded through the weeds, warm and alive, sharp enough to cut through the stink of the world. Human.

Her hackles rose at once. Every muscle in her body went rigid, ready to flee. Humans meant ropes, hands, teeth grinning with hunger. Humans meant fire barrels with no fire in them, only smoke and bone.

But this scent was different.

There was sweat, yes. Blood, faint and old. But beneath it ran something steady, solid, a heat that hooked into her chest and tugged. It pressed against a memory she couldn't hold onto: a hand brushing her fur, a voice that rumbled low, safety in the dark.

Her paws moved before she thought. She slid through the weeds, belly low, following the trail.

Every step pulled it stronger. The taste of it filled her mouth, alive and real. Not the slack meat of Slimbies, not the starving stench of hunters. This was something she hadn't felt in a year.

Hope, her body whispered, though she didn't know the word.

She crept forward, tail stiff, heart hammering, until shapes moved in the distance. A figure. Upright. Human.

She stopped dead, breath caught in her throat, the scent of him rolling thick on the wind.

He was there, not fifty paces ahead.

Alive. Moving.

She crouched low in the weeds, eyes fixed. His steps were careful, not stumbling like the dead. He paused often, scanning alleys and broken windows, the kind of looking that meant he expected danger. His hands stayed close to the strap across his shoulder where a pack hung heavy, shifting with each turn.

He didn't lurch. He didn't sway. His head turned with purpose, not hunger.

She drew his scent deep into her nose. Sweat and dirt, leather, iron. No rot. No sickness. The memory of the starving ones snapped through her. Their grins, their reaching fingers, the rope tightening around her legs. She bared her teeth at the thought, a low growl stuck in her chest.

This one was different.

She tracked every movement: the bend of his knees, the tilt of his head, the way his eyes narrowed when he scanned a corner. He was quiet, too. Almost as quiet as her. Not predator. Not prey. Something in between.

The weeds brushed her shoulders as she crept closer, paws sinking soft into the soil. Her heartbeat thudded in her ears. She knew she should vanish, fade into shadow like she always had. But something held her there, fixed to him.

When the wind shifted again, his head snapped toward her.

Their eyes met.

Her body locked tight, every muscle screaming to run. But his eyes weren't empty. Not wide and hollow like the dead. Not starved and burning like the hunters. Just tired. Sharp. Searching.

She didn't move.

The world narrowed to the space between them.

His gaze held hers, steady and unflinching. Not a predator's glare, not a starving man's hunger. Just a weight that pressed, waiting to see what she would do.

She froze, every nerve pulled tight. Ears sharp forward, tail stiff, paws dug into the dirt. One twitch from him and she'd bolt.

That was how it had always been: see a man, run before the rope, before the teeth.

But he didn't lunge.

Slowly, so slowly she tracked every inch, he bent at the knees. His body lowered toward the ground, balanced, careful, hands open where she could see them. The motion was deliberate, not the twitch of sickness or the wild flail of hunger.

He spoke. A sound low and steady, words she couldn't understand but felt in the weight of his tone. Not threat. Not shout. Just sound meant to soothe.

"It's okay. You want something to eat?"

Her ears flicked, uncertain.

The air trembled between them, her breath fogging in sharp bursts, his chest rising and falling slow. Still he didn't move closer. Still he just watched, patient, his eyes never leaving hers.

The wind carried his scent over her again. Warm. Human. Alive. It coiled through her chest, stirring memory she couldn't hold.

Her claws flexed in the dirt. She didn't run.

Then his hand moved slow, deliberate. Not toward her, but toward the pack slung across his shoulder.

Her muscles tightened. A growl rumbled low in her chest.

But he didn't pull rope, or steel, or fire. He reached in, rustled, and brought out something small. He set it down on the cracked pavement between them. A scrap of food. Meat. The scent hit her nose sharp and real, and it cut through her suspicion like a blade.

Another scrap followed, dropped a little closer to him.

"See?" he murmured. His voice was soft, coaxing. He nudged the first bit nearer with his fingertips, then drew his hand back, palm open again where she could watch.

The smell reached her in waves. Fat and salt. Her stomach twisted on itself, empty and aching, but still she held back, every muscle locked between hunger and fear.

Her eyes darted from the food to his hands, then back. His gaze stayed steady, unblinking, patient.

The scraps sat there in the dirt, waiting.

The smell clawed at her throat, rich and sharp, so close it felt like pain.

She inched forward one step. Stopped. Ears back, eyes on him. His body didn't shift, didn't twitch. Only the slow rise and fall of his chest.

Another step.

Her paw brushed the edge of the first scrap. She froze, teeth bared, a low growl curling out of her throat. If it was a trick, if his hand darted out, she would bolt and never look back.

But he didn't move.

Her tongue flicked out, quick, snatching the morsel from the ground. She chewed hard, swallowed faster. The taste lit up her chest, raw and alive.

When her eyes lifted, he was still there. Still waiting.

The second scrap lay closer to him. She paced, back and forth, every muscle a spring. Hunger dragged her forward, fear yanked her back. It became a dance. Step, stop, retreat, step again. The space between them shrank by inches.

He spoke again, quiet, steady, soft. She didn't recognize the words, only the weight of them. His hand stayed open on the dirt, palm flat, like an offering.

She crept near enough to smell the sweat on his skin. Her breath came sharp and fast, ears flicking wild.

One more step.

The second scrap was hers. She snatched it, teeth brushing his fingertips as she tore it away. The taste of salt and fat filled her mouth again. Her body trembled, torn between flight and something else she couldn't name.

Still, he didn't reach.

Still, he just waited.

Her jaws worked the scrap down in one hard swallow. She backed a step, ears flicked flat, but her eyes never left him.

His hand stayed low, open on the ground. Not grabbing. Not threatening. Just there.

She edged forward again, slow, belly low, until the space between them was little more than a breath. The smell of him was thick now. Sweat, dirt, leather, blood faint under it all. Alive.

Her nose brushed his fingers before she knew she'd moved that close. She jerked back, startled, but he didn't flinch. He only let his hand stay where it was, steady as stone.

The second time she leaned in, she didn't pull away. His fingertips grazed the fur along her cheek, rough and warm. The touch struck something buried in her chest. A memory flaring quick and painful: Noah's hand. The barn. A fire's glow.

She pressed closer without meaning to.

His hand slid gently down her neck. His fingers bumped something hard beneath the mat of her fur. The collar.

Carefully, he turned the little tag over between his thumb and forefinger. The letters caught a streak of light, dulled but still carved deep. The marker that had been there had long since faded. The only word remaining...

"...Girl," he read aloud, his voice low, almost reverent.

Her ears twitched at the sound. The word wasn't new, not really. But in his voice it felt returned, anchored again to something real.

He looked into her eyes. A tired smile pulled at his mouth, small but steady. "I'm Ben," he said softly, giving something back to her in return.

The air between them shifted. For the first time in a year, she wasn't alone.

The sound of his voice lingered in her chest, steady and strange.

Ben.

Her body trembled with the instinct to run, but the warmth of his hand still pressed against her fur. Not rough like the ones who grabbed. Not cruel like the ones who pulled. Just firm, alive, real.

She leaned into it, cautious at first, then heavier, her weight settling against him. A low whine slipped from her throat. Not warning, not fear. Something smaller. Something she hadn't made in a long time.

His hand stilled for a moment, then moved slow again, smoothing along her neck, over her shoulders. She closed her eyes halfway, ears twitching at every sound, but she didn't pull away.

For the first time since the barn, since the church, since the snow swallowed Noah's scent, she wasn't only surviving. She was here, pressed against something warm that pressed back.

Ben let out a long breath she felt more than heard. The sound wasn't hunger. It wasn't threat. It was relief.

She stayed there, body taut but no longer ready to spring, the two of them fixed in the broken street. Around them the ruins loomed, empty windows watching, wind scraping across the pavement.

But for that moment, it was only the two of them.

Not alone anymore.

About the Author

D. R. Long lives in Delaware with his dog, Girl.
He believes a story should be worth its salt; judged for its
substance rather than its aesthetic.

Find other works at **drlongwrites.com**.

MORE FROM D. R. LONG

A WORLD WE NEVER KNEW

Chance

An excerpt from the novella
by
D. R. Long

Chapter 1

Autumn rolled in like a hurricane, but she had a habit of doing that. She was always full of energy, like she had a never ending supply of internal batteries. Big energy in a little package.

"Wakey, wakey, la-zy la-dy!" she sang, skipping her way down the creaky hallway of the old farmhouse. "Better put some pants on, I'm coming in!"

She threw Nova's door open with a bang that rattled the old farmhouse, bounded across the room, and yanked the sheets down to the foot of the bed.

"The sun is up, the birds are out, and we got deer to hunt! Come on Nova, let's go!" She stood proudly at the foot of the bed waiting for Nova to move.

Nova groaned, curling her face into her arms, the light bouncing off her golden-brown skin. Her long hair tumbled across the pillow in wild curls, catching the sunlight in copper streaks.

"Five more days, please," she whined, muffled into her elbow.

Autumn gasped, pressing a hand to her chest like she'd been mortally wounded. "Five whole days? And what about poor Rusty?"

At the end of the bed, a golden retriever lifted his head from under the blankets, ears perked, eyes bright. He gave a soft wuff as if to say, You called me?

Nova peeked out with one eye, already fighting a smile, "Fine. For Rusty…"

The dog didn't need a second invitation. With a joyful grunt he launched his full weight onto Nova's side. She squealed, trying to shove him away, but Rusty pawed at her face and licked her chin until she dissolved into giggles.

Autumn walked over to the window, peeking outside then back to Nova and Rusty, grinning at the chaos she'd set loose. "See? Even Rusty knows it's hunting day. We're definitely catching something today. I can feel it!"

Nova pushed the dog off and sat up slowly, hair a storm around her face. She gave Autumn a look that was half glare, half reluctant amusement.

"One of these days, hurricane, I'm going to lock my door."

She blew a tuft of black curl out of her eye line.

Autumn tilted her head, feigning innocence, "And deprive me of the joy of saving you from eternal sleep? Not a chance."

Rusty jumped down and trotted to the door, tail wagging hard enough to thump the dresser. He barked once, sharp and eager, then padded toward the stairs like he already had his boots on. Nova groaned again, but the fight was over. The day had her now, whether she wanted it to or not.

Autumn clapped her hands. "See? That's two votes. Majority rules. Get dressed, Nova. We're losing daylight."

"But I want a shower first!" Nova whined.

Autumn turned and started walking down the hall, "Shoulda thought've that before you slept in! Outside in five!"

Autumn padded down the hallway, the boards flexing under her bare feet. The farmhouse always talked when it woke. Groans in the rafters, a sharp pop from the tin roof warming in the sun. She liked the way it sounded alive, even if Nova called it "creepy as hell."

She brushed her hand along the faded wallpaper as she passed, the flowers worn to ghosts of themselves. At the end of the hall, the stairwell yawned dark, the banister polished smooth from decades of hands.

Rusty bounded beside her, tail sweeping the floor. He barked once and fell quiet again, ears angled toward the kitchen.

Autumn paused, listening.

For a heartbeat she swore she heard something under the silence. A faint hiss, almost like an old radio trying to find a station. It was gone before she could pin it, leaving only the steady tick of the wall clock.

She shook her head and kept moving.

The stairs complained beneath her weight, each step echoing through the still house. She ducked through the low doorway into the kitchen, where sunlight spilled through lace curtains onto the scarred wooden table. Mason jars lined the shelves, some full, some empty, their labels curling at the edges.

"Coffee first," she muttered, reaching for the enamel pot on the propane stove. Rusty flopped onto the rug by the back door, but his ears stayed pricked, like he was still listening for something.

Autumn pumped the stove to life, flame catching with a hollow pop. The smell of propane mixed with the faint tang of old wood smoke embedded in the walls. She filled the pot, set it on the burner, and leaned back against the counter, arms crossed.

Nova's footsteps came overhead, slow and dragging. Autumn smirked to herself. "Four minutes," she said under her breath. "She'll be down in four."

She reached into the pantry, checking jars. Dried beans, pickled okra, half a tin of ground coffee. They'd need to get more supplies again soon, but not today. Today was for deer.

On the table lay their Boone map, corners dog-eared from folding, little circles scrawled where they'd hit stores and houses before. A hunting knife rested on top like a paperweight, still flecked with yesterday's sharpening dust.

The kettle began to hiss. Rusty's tail thumped twice, like he'd been waiting for that sound.

Autumn poured herself a mug, took a long swallow, and carried the rest out back toward the garage.

The garage smelled of oil and dust, the kind of tang that clung to everything no matter how many times Autumn cracked the windows. The teal pickup squatted in the center, hood up, its paint sun-faded to the color of old robin's eggs. A length of hose ran from the makeshift biodiesel rig to the tank, the slow gurgle of fuel almost drowned by the hiss of the burner keeping the mix warm.

Autumn leaned against the fender, mug in hand, the last inch of coffee swirling dark at the bottom. She watched the hose twitch, counted out the seconds, then pulled it free with a practiced twist. A splash hit the concrete, sharp-smelling, before she capped the tank and wiped her hand on her jeans.

She'd just taken her final sip when Nova's boots scuffed the threshold.

"Ten minutes," Autumn said without looking up. "World record. You dressing for prom up there, or just brushing each curl one at a time?"

Nova shot her a look like needles as she stepped inside, arms full of packs and gear. "Some of us believe in basic hygiene."

Autumn grinned and sniffed at her own armpits, "Did you have time to shower? I sure did!"

"Of course you did," Nova scoffed.

Rusty trotted over behind Nova, tail sweeping boxes as he went straight to sniff the fletching on her arrows. Nova set the packs on the workbench, methodical as always, and started sorting: knives, coils of rope, the bow, the rifle wrapped in oilcloth.

Autumn shut the hood with a clang, "See, that's your problem. You pack like we're leaving for a month."

"And you pack like we're walking down the street," Nova countered, sliding the bow into its case. "Better to have it and not need it."

"I know, I know, than to need it and not have it." Autumn finished the sentence for her, bobbing her head back and forth as she said it.

"If you know, why do we always have this fight?" Nova looked up from her organizing.

"The same reason one of us can't wake up in time. Better

move fast and not trip over your own baggage," Autumn shot
back, but the smile on her face softened the jab.

Rusty barked once, as if to say enough already, and padded
toward the passenger side of the truck.

Autumn slung the empty mug onto the workbench and
clapped her hands together. "Alright, let's hit it."

She swung open the driver's door, the hinges squealing their
usual complaint. Rusty bounded up first, scrambling into the
passenger seat like he owned it. He turned a circle, tail whacking
the dashboard, before settling with his nose pressed to the glass.

"Front seat's taken," Autumn said cheerfully as she climbed
in.

Nova rolled her eyes and hauled the gear across the concrete.
She stacked packs and weapons in the truck bed, cinched them
down tight with rope, then slid the bow between the seats. When
she finally climbed into the cab, she gave Rusty a shove that
barely moved him. He licked her elbow in triumph.

Autumn twisted the key. The truck coughed, sputtered, then
roared to life with a rattle that shook the rearview mirror. Blue
smoke belched from the exhaust. She patted the dash. "See?
Smooth as silk."

"Silk that's been dragged through a junkyard," Nova
muttered, buckling her belt.

The garage door groaned upward, spilling pale morning light across the hood. Beyond, the dirt track ran down to the road, grass pushing up through the gravel. Fields stretched beyond that, rimmed with forest already gone wild at the edges.

Autumn eased the truck into gear, ties crunching over the floor's grit, and rolled them out into the open air. The farmhouse shrank behind them as they bumped down the drive. White paint peeling, porch slouched, lace curtains glowing faint in the sun. For just a second, the rocking chair on the porch creaked forward, though no wind stirred.

Nova glanced back, lips pressing thin. Autumn caught it, but kept her eyes on the road.

Rusty whined once, nose already working as the truck turned toward Boone.

Chapter 2

The 1950's model pickup rattled down the back roads, every loose bolt and dented panel joining in its own chorus. Autumn hunched forward over the wheel, one hand drumming a rhythm against the dash, the other steadying their lurching path through potholes and overgrown cracks in the asphalt.

Kudzu had swallowed the fence lines, dragging whole mailboxes into green cocoons. A rusted tractor set nose-deep in weeds, its tires long gone. The world wasn't empty, it was being reclaimed.

Rusty rode shotgun with his nose jammed into the half-cracked vent window. His ears twitched constantly, little radar dishes tuning for scents. Every few minutes he gave a short, satisfied huff, as if confirming to himself what was out there.

"Out by noon, home by dusk," Nova said from the passenger side, her eyes sweeping the tree line. She said it like she was checking boxes on a list, the same way she always did when they left the farmhouse.

Autumn grinned without looking over. "Yeah, yeah. I know the rules."

They passed a sun-bleached county sign pointing one way toward Boone and the other toward the city. Rusty's ears snapped forward at the city. A low growl rumbled in his chest, so soft it barely carried over the engine noise.

Autumn reached out and tapped the dashboard twice with her knuckles, a superstitious habit as automatic as breathing. Nova noticed but didn't comment.

The road curved past an old school bus tilted on its axles, paint flaking like scabs. Autumn downshifted, and the truck rattled as they rolled by. Neither spoke. Both listened.

At first, only the sounds of the biodiesel engine rumbling. Faintly, almost inaudible, a brief dream-like sound of screams from children playing on the bus.

"Hurry up, Autumn," Nova said, her eyes narrowing on the bus. "I hate it when it's kids."

When the road straightened again, the valley ahead opened wide. Boone's square came into view. Quiet buildings, a single street cutting through, the outlines of their little rituals waiting.

Autumn leaned her elbow out the window, a grin creeping across her face.

"Can we stop in town," she made puppy dog eyes at Nova. "Pwease?"

Nova tried to hide a smile, "Only if there's pancakes for us."

"Yes!" Autumn's eyes lit up. "And maybe there'll be fresh strawberries!"

Boone was a hushed little mountain town, tucked between low green ridges. Two-story brick storefronts lined the square, their windows sun-faded and blank. A coffee shop, a hardware store, a bookstore, all still standing like props on a stage after the actors had gone. Side streets branched off into neighborhoods where porches slouched and grass pressed up through cracked pavement. The mountains leaned close on every side, holding the town in a quiet, airless bowl.

The pickup groaned to a stop in front of the café, tires crunching on gravel that had already started to sprout weeds. The chalkboard sign in the window still read Cold Brew Today, though the chalk had faded nearly white.

Autumn swung down from the cab, jingling the door chime with more force than necessary when she pushed inside. "Morning, y'all," she called out to the empty shop, same as always.

Rusty stayed planted at the threshold. His tail wagged, but his nose kept sweeping low and fast across the seam of the door. He gave a sharp sniff, then sat, waiting for the all clear.

Outside, tall grass grew through the cracks in the sidewalk. And the faint sounds of distant memories echoed in the streets. The sound of a jump rope hitting the concrete, a paper boy calling out headlines, the hustle and bustle of what once was a busy small town.

Inside, the place smelled of dust and lingering coffee grounds. The faintly humming cooler still held a row of glass pitchers, condensation streaking down the glass. Nova went straight to the counter, dropped a couple of bills into the tip jar that already held their old deposits, edges curled from time. Autumn added her own, lighter, almost tossed in like she was playing a game.

"Make sure you tip," Autumn called out. "Can't cheat the dead."

Nova's mouth pressed into the ghost of a smile as she wiped a ring of dust off the counter with her sleeve. "They're not dead, they're just…gone."

"Same thing!"

Behind the café, a weathered picket fence wrapped around a small patch of earth like it belonged to an old house more than a shop. The garden had gone half-wild, but rows of herbs and berry plants still clung to order. Nova slipped out the back door and wandered through the garden. She knelt in the dirt, brushing aside weeds to pluck strawberries, their skins bright against her dusty palms. Rusty nosed between the posts, tail wagging as if keeping watch.

Inside, Autumn had dragged out a propane canister and coaxed the café stove to life with a sputtering pop. She whistled tunelessly while she worked, mixing batter from flour and powdered milk, splashing water from their jug. The skillet hissed as she dropped the first ladleful, the smell of frying batter blooming into the quiet shop.

Nova came in with her shirt hem cradling the berries. "This should be enough!"

"Perfect," Autumn said, crushing a few straight into the bowl. "House special."

They ate at the counter with enamel mugs of cold brew, plates balanced on stacks of old menus. Rusty sprawled across both their boots, licking at crumbs that fell his way. For a few minutes, with sunlight pouring through the lace curtains and the garden framed outside, Boone felt less like a ghost town and more like home.

Nova cleared the dishes into a sink and began washing them off. Autumn sat at the bar fiddling with a radio knob out of habit. A hiss, a crackle, something almost like a cough of static voices, and then nothing. She snapped it off again, jaw tight.

"Still dead," she said too quickly. "Just once I'd like some old tunes."

Nova didn't answer, setting dishes into a strainer beside the sink.

Rusty gave a short, impatient whine from the doorway.

"Alright, alright," Autumn said, draining her cup. "He's got a schedule to keep."

"Thank you for breakfast." Nova smiled.

"Thank you for the company," Autumn shot a wink back.

They stepped back into the sunlight. Boone's square lay quiet ahead, waiting.

The bell above the bookstore door didn't ring anymore, but Autumn gave it a flick on her way in, just to hear the faint clink. Dust hung in the air, cut by narrow shafts of sunlight that slipped through warped blinds.

Rusty padded inside, claws ticking against the cuffed wood floor. He flopped in a bright rectangle of sunlight near the front, his chest rising and falling with a deep, dog-heavy sigh.

Their "swap shelf" waited against the back wall: a short bookcase they'd cleared months ago, filled now with worn spines they'd rotated in and out. A notebook sat on top, open to their last entry.

Nova went straight for the shelves. She pulled a field guide to southeastern plants, flipping through the index with a quick hand, then dog-eared a page. Next she took a thin medical text, sliding a scrap of paper between chapters on sutures. Finally, a rope-work manual, its cover half torn away. She stacked them neatly at her side, efficient as always.

Autumn wandered slower, fingertips trailing along cracked spines. She plucked out a battered poetry collection, flipped to the first page, and smiled faintly at the underlined lines inside. Someone else's ghost of taste. Next she chose a novel with a sun-faded jacket promising a triumphant story of love and survival. She dug a pencil from her pocket and scribbled inside the cover: This one's good!

On the lower shelf, her hand stopped on a children's picture book. The cover was bright still, a bear in a red scarf. She held it for a moment longer than the others, then slid it back, her jaw tightening.

Rusty rose before either of them said a word. He stretched, yawned wide, then nudged the door open with his nose.

"Boss says we're done," Autumn said tucking her finds under her arm.

Nova glanced once around the shop, then closed the ledger. "Let's move."

They stepped back into the square, the silence waiting for them.

The hardware store's front window was cracked from corner to corner, a white spiderweb of glass that hadn't yet given way. Autumn gave it a testing knock with her knuckle as they slipped inside. The air was dry, metallic like rusty nails and dust.

Rows of shelves stood half-stripped. A few still held lonely items: boxes of screws, duct tape rolls, a tangle of extension cords. Nova moved aisle to aisle with a quiet precision, pulling what they actually needed: a coil of rope, a small tin of gun oil, a single box of rifle rounds. She checked each item, held it to the light, then set it neatly into her pack.

Autumn disappeared for a minute and came back grinning, a roll of duct tape in each hand. She immediately tore off a strip and slapped it across the crack in the truck's glove box outside the door.

"There. Much better!" She put her hands on her hips and gave a firm nod, admiring her handy work.

Nova arched an eyebrow. "Proud of yourself?"

"Sure am!" Autumn shot back with a smirk.

At the counter, Nova found a scrap of paper and a pushpin. She scrawled their note in blunt letters:
TAKE WHAT YOU NEED. LEAVE WHAT YOU CAN. -A+N

She pinned it to the dusty corkboard behind the register where old community fliers still curled.

Autumn leaned over the counter, eyeing the scrawled dance-lesson poster beneath it. "Think we missed our class," she said.

"Shame," Nova murmured, shouldering her pack, "I really could use some new moves."

Rusty padded through the aisles, tail brushing low, and gave a single short bark from the doorway.

Back in the truck, Nova pulled a grease-stained index card from the glove box and ticked off each item with a stub of pencil. Autumn drummed her fingers on the steering wheel, already itching to move.

"Supply run complete," Nova said.

"Next stop, the great outdoors," Autumn replied, and turned the key.

The only gas station was on the edge of Boone. It sagged under its own roof, one awning beam splintered but somehow still holding. Autumn eased the truck to a stop, gravel popping under the tires. When the engine cut, the silence that followed felt heavier than the rattling ride in.

Rusty lifted his head from the window, ears sweeping the lot like radar. After a moment, he huffed once and relaxed, but his eyes stayed on the tree line beyond the pumps.

Nova spread the Boone map across her knees, the corners worn soft from folding. She traced their route with a finger, voice quiet but certain. "Up the creek bed, loop south, back by mid afternoon. If anything slows us…" She tapped a dotted fallback line.

Autumn handed her the dented thermos from the cup holder. Nova passed her a granola bar in return. The ritual exchange. Never spoken, always done.

They climbed out together. Packs were lifted, straps cinched, weapons checked. Nova ran her thumb across the bowstring, listening for the taut hum. Autumn slid her rifle over one shoulder, then stepped back to give the truck two solid knocks on the hood.

"Good luck, old girl," she muttered.

The woods waited past the overgrown lot, pines leaning into one another, their shade swallowing the gravel road.

"I love the silence out here," Nova said, folding the map and tucking it away. "Makes me forget about everyone being gone."

Autumn met her eyes, nodded once, and led the first step off the road and into the trees. "Funny…everyone's gone, and the woods are still the quietest place."

Rusty padded ahead, tail high, the forest swallowing them whole.

Dive deeper into the Spiral - scan the code below!